MW00622625

BE FAST
OR
BE GONE

BE FAST
OR
BE GONE

Racing the Clock with
Critical Chain Project Management

Andreas Scherer

ProChain Press

Publisher's Cataloging-in-Publication
(Provided by Quality Books, Inc.)
Scherer, Andreas, 1964–
        Be fast or be gone : racing the clock with critical
    chain project management / by Andreas Scherer.
        p. cm.
        LCCN 2010940389
        ISBN 13: 978-1-934979-07-5 (hardcover)
        ISBN 13: 978-1-934979-08-2 (ebook)
        1. Brain--Cancer--Patients--Fiction. 2. Brain--
    Cancer--Fiction. 3. Drug development--Fiction.
    4. Project management--Fiction. I. Title.
    PS3619.C3495B4 2011   813'.6
                               QBI10-600255

Cover and interior stopwatch photo: iStock©Bibigon. Photo manipulation by RD Studio.

Book design by DesignForBooks.com

Printed in the United States of America

CONTENTS

PREFACE

*L*ong before Henry Ford figured out how to make more cars in less time by using the assembly line, the business world wanted to be faster. Be fast and you get your product to customers sooner. Be fast and you have a winning edge over your competition. Be fast and you increase your bottom line.

Executives know that the demand for speed never stops. Like competitors in the 100-yard dash, we always want to shave just a little bit more off our best time, and then shave a little more off of that. Businesses want to be faster, because otherwise someone else will be there first. Yet most companies struggle to figure out how to do it. No matter what they do, projects seem to come in late, and everything takes just a little longer than expected.

Over the many years that we have been implementing Critical Chain solutions in Fortune 500 companies, we have helped them to substantially improve their on-time delivery performance. Companies that have correctly learned to use Critical Chain are typically on time with more than ninety-five percent of their projects. More than that, we have successfully accelerated those projects, cutting up to fifty percent off their historical project durations.

These numbers sound too good to be true. They're not. But it's hard to believe in the Critical Chain approach until you've seen it at work. I spend a lot of time talking to executives about Critical Chain. I go over the mechanics and the underlying principles. I give people case studies. I have them do group exercises. I write blogs. But I found that no matter how much I talked about Critical Chain and no matter how well I did it, you can't really get it until you've seen it applied. I wrote this book because I wanted you to have the opportunity to see Critical Chain at work, in an imaginary company, the way that it has worked for our Fortune 500 customers and the way that it could work for you.

The story is fiction. There is no Mike Knight and there is no Altus Labs. But the details in their story are taken from my experiences implementing the Critical Chain in companies all over the world.

Above all, this story will introduce you to the three simple concepts at the heart of Critical Chain:

- Sound project planning
- Disciplined execution of key tasks
- Focused work that lets your people get the job done

Be Fast or Be Gone shows you how these simple principles are applied on an individual project and throughout an organization. It shows you what happens when the principles aren't in place, and it shows you how fast change can happen when they are. It shows you how you can leverage Critical Chain in your efforts to continuously get better and more competitive. It shows you the way to become a market leader.

ANDREAS SCHERER
January, 2011
Lake Ridge, Virginia

ACKNOWLEDGMENTS

*R*ob Newbold and Bill Lynch founded ProChain Solutions, a Critical Chain Project Management Company, in 1996. They created the relationships with major companies and drove the development of ProChain's software and processes that have led to the company's long-standing record of success. They started ProChain Press. Without their hard work and entrepreneurial spirit, this book never could have been written. Without their extremely valuable advice during the various iterations of *Be Fast or Be Gone*, this would have been a much different book. I owe them many thanks.

I am also grateful to my other colleagues at ProChain for their continuous efforts to improve Critical Chain Project Management. In particular, Bill Fulton, Dr. Richard Moore, and Dr. Wendell Simpson were very supportive of this book and provided useful feedback.

Be Fast or Be Gone describes the implementation of Critical Chain at Altus Labs—a fictional pharmaceutical company based in the Philadelphia area. I received a lot of input from people in the life sciences industry that helped me make this fictional company feel more real. In particular I'd like to thank Jason Bork, Jesse Conard, Dr. Hugh Davis, David Douglas, Dr. Martin Hynes, Ann Gerritsen, Dr. Eric Morfin, Dr. Sandra Morris, and Dr. John Sun for lending me their expertise.

In addition, I received help from people who are very close to the world of Critical Chain and process improvement. I'd like to thank Dr. Steve Eppinger, Dr. Chip Heath, Dr. James Holt, Nancy Malthouse, and Maike Scherer for their invaluable comments.

And finally, a big "thank you" goes out to Dr. Sarah Skwire. She lent me her expertise as the author of *Writing with a Thesis* and her experience as a writer to guide me through this project.

Chapter 1

BAD NEWS

*I*t had been a long time since anyone had made Mike Knight wait for anything. He made all his business trips with the same airline so that, with his platinum status, he never had to wait to get onto the plane. He never checked luggage, of course. Why wait at baggage claim when you could just learn to pack a little smarter and save yourself forty-five minutes? He went to the same Starbucks every morning on his way into the office because his favorite barista already knew that he wanted his double-shot cappuccino extra dry and with non-fat milk. He didn't have to waste time ordering. Most mornings the cup was ready for him before he'd even gotten to the front of the line to pay. He listened to executive summaries of the most important business books on his phone while he did his morning workout. He had his admin schedule his business calls as if they were thirty-minute meetings so he didn't get caught up in long conversations about weekend golf, soccer coaching, and the newest brew pub. He never let email sit in his in-box overnight. By the end of the day, a message was filed, deleted, or answered. If he could find a way to be more efficient, he did it. If he could shave five minutes off an errand, he would.

Even Timmy, who wanted to be called Tim now that he had reached the sophisticated age of eight, had been born early. Mike's wife joked that any child of his would have known better than to be late. Dad wouldn't stand for it.

Saving time, managing time, creating time where no one thought it existed, that's what Mike did. That's how he made his living, and he was good at it. Very good. So when Mike Knight's world started to crumble around him, it was made all the worse because it started so damn slowly.

◆◆◆

It had begun early that March when Tim began sleeping late most mornings. Then he got a little klutzier than he ever had been on the soccer field. Mike and Sally attributed it all to growing pains and to one of those phases kids go through where you can see the annoying teenager that your darling grade-schooler will grow up to be.

A few weeks later he started to get headaches. Allergies, they thought, or maybe a sinus infection. Or maybe he just needed glasses. They made an appointment with the optometrist to have his eyes examined.

It was one night after a soccer practice in April, as he lay sprawled on the couch watching television, that he had the seizure. Mike and Sally, terrified, had taken him to the ER, which sent them directly to a staff neurologist. He'd admitted Tim, ordered an MRI, and then called Mike and Sally into his office while Tim slept quietly in a room on the children's floor.

In silent fear, they sat and waited for him to explain what was happening.

Dr. Maples sat with Tim's chart open on his desk. Several times he seemed on the point of speaking but then looked down at the chart again. Finally, he simply handed them one of the scans from the MRI.

There it was, on the left side of their son's brain, his perfect, smart, funny, inquisitive, fascinating, curious little brain. A black, ominous splotch.

"Is that . . . ? Does Tim have a . . . ? My god, Mike, I can't even say it."

Mike swallowed his rising nausea and panic. "Are you telling us that our son has a brain tumor?"

Dr. Maples nodded slowly. "I'm sorry. This isn't the kind of news you ever get used to delivering. There's no good way to tell you, but this looks very bad. Tim obviously has a brain tumor, and it's large and, I think, fairly advanced."

"So what are our options?"

"There are a few things we can try, some standard approaches that may prove helpful. Tumors are hard to predict. We don't see a lot of them in children Tim's age. We haven't got a lot of data to work with on this kind of thing.

"What all that means is that, while I can tell you what we can expect if we don't do anything about this tumor . . ."

"Like what?"

Mike had never seen his wife look so pale and terrified. Not the time they had to rush Tim to the emergency room because he'd broken his collarbone. Not the time they'd stayed up all night with a sixth-month-old Tim during his first bout of stomach flu. Not even the time when, for what had previously been the worst ten minutes of Mike's life, they lost track of Tim at the playground. Those ten minutes, bad as they were, had dissolved in relief and joy when they found him sitting behind a tree trying to persuade a squirrel to come home to live with him. But these minutes, here and now—Mike was beginning to understand, looking at Dr. Maples's solemn face, looking at his wife's frightened one, that this wasn't going to be solved as easily as finding a lost little boy on a playground.

"If we don't find a way to treat the tumor then it will grow, spread, and put a lot of pressure on his brain. The pressure causes the symptoms we are already seeing. They will get worse."

Mike could feel Sally's cold fingers reaching for his. He knew she was thinking, like he was, of all the times recently that they'd scolded Tim for being scatterbrained, for not listening, not paying attention, not behaving in class. They'd been scolding him, telling him to shape up or he'd lose TV and Internet privileges, and he was sick.

"What I want to do is send Tim to Bethesda to see a specialist in pediatric oncology. Her name is Dr. Hart, and she works with the National Cancer Institute. She's seen a lot more of this than I have and she'll know all your best options. There are one or two people you could work with locally, but if you can manage the trip, Dr. Hart is who I'd take my own children to see."

Later, Sally told Mike she didn't remember how they got out of the office. She didn't remember the drive home either, didn't remember calling Dr. Hart to make an appointment, didn't remember bursting into tears when the nurse told her there was a one-week wait to see the doctor. But Mike remembered that. He remembered every minute of those precious days slipping away from him, slipping away from Tim, as they waited. And waited. And waited.

Bethesda, Maryland, is right outside of Washington, D.C. They had tried to make the trip to the capital into a little family vacation. They toured the monuments, hit the Air and Space Museum, and logged a lot of time in the hotel pool. But through it all they were waiting. Waiting to see the doctor. Waiting for the test techs to be ready. Waiting for the biopsy results to come in. Waiting for Dr. Hart to have a look at the results. And waiting for a chance to meet with her.

Mike had gone back to see Dr. Hart alone, to hear about the results. He and Sally wanted Tim to hear the news, whatever it was, from them. They wanted to have a chance to try to understand it for themselves first, before they tried to explain it to Tim.

Dr. Hart didn't have any good news. There really couldn't be good news for the parents of a kid with a brain tumor. Anything other than "Oops. We misread the tests, he's fine" is a disaster. And she hadn't said that. She hadn't said anything close.

"Mr. Knight, it's not good news. The biopsy we did confirms that your son has, at best, a rare kind of malignant tumor called an anaplastic astrocytoma. I said "at best" because these biopsies only test a small portion of the tumor. And tumors can be heterogeneous. The part that's tested can present as one kind of tumor, while another part that the biopsy didn't let us look at can be another kind. So the anaplastic astrocytoma is our best of the bad options. There's a possibility that Tim's tumor is a glioblastoma. That's . . . that's as bad as news can get, I'm afraid. And I think that, to be safe, we need to proceed as if a glioblastoma is what he has. That means he needs radical treatment, and quickly."

Mike sat, sick and unmoving, hardly able to follow the barrage of technical information, no matter how clear and gentle Dr. Hart was trying to be.

"The survival rates for these types of tumors . . . frankly, they're not very good. But here's what you need to remember. If you ask me about statistics on tumors like this, and what they mean for Tim, here's the problem. Give me a group of four hundred people in Tim's situation and I can give you some percentages, some survival rates at four months, six months, eighteen months. But if you ask me about your child, I have to say that I just don't know. Tim is one child, with his own medical history, his own strengths, and his own weaknesses. We have to treat him, not the statistics.

"There is, though, some slightly better news hiding here. Tim's tumor appears to be limited to his brain's left hemisphere. That means it has a surgical success rate of about forty percent. If he had a mid-line tumor that spread between both hemispheres, the odds would be about half that.

"Now, surgery can only go so far and only do so much before it damages the brain more than it helps it. But we can address this with tools other than surgery. We'll do that, of course, and as quickly as we can. After the surgery, we'll begin an aggressive course of radiation therapy, which will shrink but not eliminate the tumor. There are also drugs we can use that will help, but won't beat this. You have to realize that Tim's tumor is at stage three. That means the prognosis is simply not very good. We'll throw everything we have at it, though, and then we're just going to have to wait and see."

Why did every doctor in the world tell patients to wait and see? There had to be something else. There was always something to do, something better than just waiting. There's always a solution. You just have to look harder. That's what Mike always told the guys who worked for him, and he believed it.

"There has to be something else, Dr. Hart. So far you're talking about fairly conventional treatment. What about experimental surgery? A drug trial? Someone must have something in development, right? It's the twenty-first century."

"Believe me, Mr. Knight. I feel the same way you do. That's why I'm in this line of work. But there's nothing . . ."

She paused. Mike knew that pause. That was the pause he got when one of the guys on his team was insisting that a problem couldn't be solved, that nothing could be done, and realized halfway through the protests that maybe, just maybe, it could be.

"What? You have to understand, I will do anything for my son. I'm lucky enough to be able to fly him anywhere for a surgery, to be able to pay for any kind of medication, to . . . I'll do anything. Just help him. Please."

She sighed slowly. "There's a drug, Mr. Knight. It's in the earliest stages of development at Altus Labs. It's called Supragrel. My friend Charlene Palmer is Vice-President of Project Management over at Altus. She also chairs the governance committee that oversees this kind of drug development project. She tells me that Supragrel is meant to treat exactly this type of tumor in kids exactly like your son. But it's only in Phase I of testing. The drug has shown some promising results with adults, but using it on children is uncharted territory. Now, Tim would qualify for inclusion in a study of this drug, and when Supragrel is ready for Phase II testing I should be able to get him in. But I don't know when that will be. I'm going to do all I can to keep your son alive so he can be in that test group. We're going to pursue all the standard treatments—we'll have to do that anyway, to qualify him for the testing—and we're just going to have to wait and see how he does. And we're going to have to wait and see when Supragrel hits Phase II. But we're going to need to be very lucky. The timing really doesn't look good."

"Do you know what I do for a living Dr. Hart?"

"I have no idea, but why . . ."

"I work for a company called Versa. I speed up their research and development projects. I'm not going to bother you with the details. But if you could introduce me to Ms. Palmer, maybe I could help."

"I can make the introduction, I suppose. But I can't promise she'll even want to talk to you at all, much less let you have anything to do with the project. I'll do what I can. But, please, don't pin all your hopes on this. Creating and testing a new drug takes a lot of time. And time is something Tim hasn't got a lot of right now."

Chapter 2

GETTING IN

*I*t was the middle of May and Mike was waiting again. He was even doing his waiting in an official waiting room. It was a luxurious room, with deep leather couches and chairs, in the glossy, beautifully designed main office building on the Altus Labs campus in Chesterton, Pennsylvania. Chesterton was a cozy little town outside of Philadelphia, and the enormous building, the whole campus in fact, looked like it had been dropped in from outer space. Surrounded by woods, the sleek glass and brick structure spoke quietly but emphatically of money and success. The large plate-glass windows let sunlight and views of the trees into the waiting room. Ordinarily he wouldn't object to sitting quietly here for a few minutes.

But today his mind wouldn't quiet down. He couldn't stop replaying the discussion he'd had with Sally last night before he left for the airport.

"Do you really think it's going to work, Mike? Usually when you show up to pitch Critical Chain it's because you've been invited by people who already know they've got a problem. This time you're sort of dropping in to say, 'Hey, your company has problems. You don't know it. Let me fix it for you!'"

"I know. But, Sal, every company I've ever known has had timing problems. Almost everyone is always running later than they want to be. And I've got to think that the same thing is true for the big drug companies. It's got to be more true, really, with all the regulations and testing and uncertainty they have to deal with. There has to be some time I can shave off."

"I hope you're right. And I've seen you do it. Nobody knows your numbers better than I do. We'll hold things together here, and I'll cross my fingers."

Dr. Hart's call to Charlene Palmer had gotten Tim on the wait list for the Supragrel trial. When Charlene, prompted by Dr. Hart's suggestion, reviewed Tim's file, she made a subdued call to Mike to say that while Tim was a perfect subject for the study, none of the doctors she consulted expected that the drug would be ready in time to help him at all.

More determined than ever to get a look inside Altus and find a way to speed them along, Mike followed up with some more emails and a copy of his curriculum vitae. A few more phone conversations, longer and more involved, had followed. Those had led to an invitation to come into Altus to chat today, just to see what he had to offer.

"You can come in now, Mr. Knight."

Stepping into the gleaming conference room, Mike wished he felt a little less like an idiot when he wore a suit. He used to wear them every day, but Versa had become more relaxed.

"It's nice to meet you, Mike. I always like to have a face to go with the voice. I was so sorry to hear that your son is sick . . . I hope we can help him."

Mike nodded his thanks. He hadn't spoken to anyone outside his immediate family about Tim's illness, and he wasn't sure he'd be able to just yet. Fortunately, Dr. Hart had explained Tim's situation and the extraordinary interest Mike took in Supragrel when she'd spoken to Charlene about him, and Charlene had seen Tim's file. Mike wouldn't have to say anything. She already knew it all.

"I have to tell you that your credentials are really impressive, and I always like to meet people that Tamara—

sorry, I mean Dr. Hart—says are interesting. But what really got me intrigued is this report that you were able to significantly reduce cycle times in your current company. It says here that you cut more than thirty-five percent. That's a fairly impressive number. Mind telling me how you did that?"

Mike smiled. He could tell she didn't really believe him. But he loved to talk about his work, and he loved to see the lights turn on inside people when he showed them how it could work for them. With Tim's future riding on this conversation, he'd better make Charlene Palmer light up, and fast.

"I got those numbers at Versa by using a project management methodology called Critical Chain. It's based on approaches originally used in the manufacturing world. What we've done is adapt it to help knowledge workers get research and development projects done faster and more effectively. We work with cross-functional teams to develop aggressive project plans, and we use a rigorous execution process that minimizes the chances that small things will fall between the cracks. Projects are never late because one big thing goes wrong. They're late because . . . well, it's the death by a thousand cuts. It's all the small stuff, added up."

Charlene cocked an eyebrow, "I've certainly seen the problem before. But I still don't see where you save the time."

"During the planning phase we look for two things. First, tasks or sequences of tasks that can be worked in parallel instead of in series. That's a huge source of speed. Second, we try to find the true touch time for individual tasks—that's the hands-on time that it takes to get something done. Once we have that we're able to come up with much more compact project schedules.

"We also model the resources required to get the work done. This lets us find the longest chain of tasks that takes task and resource constraints into account. That is the Critical Chain. Then we work to shorten it. If your team has identified the shortest possible Critical Chain, it has found the fastest way to get a project done. We combine that with a week-to-week update process that turns that plan into reality. That's how we saved thirty-five percent of our cycle time at Versa."

"Tell me a little more about the execution process."

"Every week we identify those specific tasks that could delay the whole project schedule. We call them "Critical Chain" tasks. By definition these tasks drive the timeline. We ask any person working on one of these Critical Chain tasks to work on it with as much focus as possible. That increases the speed with which we can move the results of that particular task to the next person in line. The best part is that the clear focus and priorities that come from the schedules can help dramatically reduce multitasking, which means everyone can be faster and more efficient. It's almost like a relay race for knowledge workers."

She smiled. "I like that relay race analogy. We could use that kind of focused speed here. And it sounds like it's worked for Versa's semiconductors. But if you reduce the time in a schedule, won't that make it more susceptible to unexpected delays? We want things to go fast, but predictability is important to us."

Mike nodded. "You're always going to have stuff that comes up, problems you didn't anticipate. What we do is take some of that time we took from the individual tasks and give it back to the overall schedule. We call it a 'buffer.' It's safety time that protects the whole project, not just one person or department. When you make safety time explicit like that, and when you share it out through the whole project, you can manage it and use it where it's needed. Critical Chain schedules provide fantastic on-time performance."

Charlene had more questions.

"Okay, so we're running a race and the goal is to cross the finish line first, no matter what. Does that mean we potentially risk quality?"

"No. If anything, we found at Versa that quality increases with this approach. We want people to focus on their essential tasks. We want them to get it right the first time. Doing things that way avoids expensive rework. Prior to Critical Chain we found that people had to do a lot of rework, because they weren't focused. Redoing something is like running the same lap twice in one race. You'll never win that way."

"Faster projects that are more predictable? You'll forgive me, but that sounds too good to be true. So, I'm looking for the potential problems. It's what I do. Is it really something that could work in any business environment? Because the pharmaceutical industry has some fairly specialized requirements."

"I'm sure this could work for you. The principles are pretty fundamental. It's really just about improving the speed and consistency with which projects get executed. I don't see why it shouldn't work anywhere else. It's not specific to the semiconductor industry or to the manufacturers who started it. It's just about learning to run the race more effectively. That's what I focus on."

She nodded thoughtfully, offered him another cup of coffee, and sat in silence while he added a little cream. He stirred it in carefully, taking a little time. He hoped he'd said enough. He hoped he hadn't said too much. He allowed himself, for a just a moment, to think about the new picture of Tim he'd stuck into the pocket of his jacket this morning. Glancing up at Charlene, he could practically hear her running the numbers.

"Thirty-five percent cycle-time reduction would mean we could get a drug out in eight years instead of in twelve. That's unheard of, and I find it hard to believe that's possible, not with just a little bit of messing around with our scheduling. But let's say I'm interested in finding out more. How would we go about it?"

"Charlene, I want to be up front with you. You've seen the file and talked to Dr. Hart. You know the reason I'm interested in helping you go faster is because I want Supragrel for my son. So, give me two weeks. Let me get a close look at your processes, interview your team, and create an initial project schedule. I call it a network build. I would need the team to be all together in a room for about three days. We'll look into every corner of your processes. Then I can tell you what's possible here at Altus and what's not. We can find out if we can get Supragrel to Phase II faster. It's good for both of us."

Charlene thought about this for a moment.

"I can give you that, but we'd have to bring you in officially as a contractor, and you'd have to go through our standard on-boarding procedures. I can expedite that. But, let me be clear, if this goes any further than these initial two weeks, I'm going have to get approval for your involvement from the governance committee because of your obvious conflict-of-interest issues."

Charlene walked Mike over to HR to set up the two-week contract. Two hours later Mike left Altus Labs' headquarters. He called into the office on his way to the airport and let them know he'd be unexpectedly burning a little vacation time. Then he called Sally and simply said: "We're on our way!"

LEARNING
FROM THE INSIDE

*B*ack at Versa, Mike had always started his week running. By 6 P.M. on Sunday night he would have a report on the entire Versa project pipeline in his email. He read and reviewed it before coming into the office at 8 A.M. on Monday morning, catching his team by email, phone, or face-to-face in his office first thing to go over any surprises in the pipeline. They'd note what was running ahead of schedule, what was lagging behind, and catch any unexpected deviations from the plans they had created for a project at its onset.

By the first status meeting of the week—always at 9 A.M. every Monday—Mike and his team had been ready to talk about how to move ahead on projects that were moving well, how to mitigate problems with projects that were off-track, and general questions of process improvement. By 10 A.M., they were up-to-speed, energized, already solving the problems for the week, and ready for another cup of coffee and a quick debate about whether to get sushi or Thai food for lunch.

Altus Labs started slower.

Mike's first meeting for his first week of contracting at Altus, a briefing on the status of the early stage drug pipeline, wasn't scheduled until 11 A.M. That meant that even after he'd found the coffee machine, unpacked his office a bit, and set up his email account, he had nearly two and a half hours of downtime before he could get started on anything. Though it was only scheduled to last an hour, the meeting was obviously an important start to the week, and Mike was looking forward to the rapid uptake of new information he was sure the briefing would supply. Until then, though, he had a little time to himself, so he closed his office door and called Dr. Hart for an update on Tim.

"Oh, Mr. Knight, I'm glad that you called. We've gotten Tim's next set of test results back, and you and Sally were at the top of my list of calls to make today. The tests have given us a much better sense of the speed with which Tim's tumor is growing. Unfortunately, it's growing quickly. That means that I want to get him in for surgery as soon as possible. We want to keep that tumor from creating more pressure in his head and causing further impact on his motor coordination and on his personality."

Mike took a deep breath. The news wasn't any different than they'd had before but there was something horrible about hearing it stated so bluntly, about talking to a doctor to set a date for brain surgery for his son.

"So what's our timeline here?"

"I'd like to have him in here for surgery within the next two weeks. That will give you and your wife a little time to prepare him mentally, but I really don't think we can let it go any longer than that. After surgery, we'll start radiation therapy right away. That will take four to six months. I will try to get access to Supragrel, and I know that you're trying from your end of things, but I doubt it will be ready for a Phase II trial. As soon as it is available I'll switch him to that therapy. In the meantime, we will try to keep the cancer in check with conventional methods. We won't heal him, but the surgery will get rid of most of the tumor and the radiation may possibly prevent further growth. Most likely we can slow the spread of the cancer."

"So, we can count on about six months with this approach?"

"I never like to say that we can count on anything, Mr. Knight. Six months on the outside. Realistically, we need to evaluate the situation after four months. "

"Where would the treatment be? Will we have to move him to Bethesda for it?

"Let me look into that for you. I would rather have him stay where he is right now. Dr. Maples and I are in correspondence. I will have to conduct the surgery myself, and I'd be willing to fly out for that so that the radiation can start right away in the Santa Clara hospital."

Mike could live with that. After his sudden decision to head cross-country for two weeks, he couldn't imagine telling Sally that she and Tim would need to move to Bethesda for treatment. He was also sure that Tim would be happier in California, near his friends and all his familiar things. They said their goodbyes, and Dr. Hart promised to give Sally a call to set the surgery date and answer any questions she had.

〰〰

Mike sat in the conference room, waiting. It was already ten minutes past the scheduled start time and several of the key members of the management team hadn't made it to the meeting yet. Feeling like he was back in high school, he sat in the back of the room with Bob Gabriel, a Senior Project Manager, talking movies, new technology, and martial arts, waiting for the meeting to get going. When it did, the lights were dimmed, the AV screen lowered, and the presenter put up a slide showing the status of all Phase I and Phase II drugs. The presenter, Chad from portfolio management, started hurriedly flipping through slides as quickly as possible. Mike could barely keep up, but since the presenter promised they'd all be getting a copy of the presentation in their email by the end of the day, he didn't even bother to take notes. He couldn't help wondering why Altus didn't get that material to people before the meeting, though, so they could all avoid wasting their time silently watching slides that merely repeated information they could process on their own.

Chad then began to move through each drug development project one at a time. For each drug he announced the milestone date and then asked the functions—toxicology, regulatory, manufacturing, medical, and project management—if they were still on track to deliver by this date. His questions were mostly met by a silence that Mike assumed meant that there was no news to report and by the quiet clicking that Mike recognized as the sound of text messages being sent while the presenter flipped through slide after slide.

After about thirty minutes—Mike's feet were beginning to fall asleep—they finally got to Supragrel. Mike leaned forward in his chair, eager for details, but anxious about the bad news he suspected was waiting for him.

"Let's move on to Supragrel. We are in the tail end of Phase I. The adult study reports are still on track to complete by their milestone date, September 1st of this year. About three months from now. We need to collect the data, write up a report, obtain approval from the governance committee, and move into Phase II. Our milestone for First Patient Visit of our Phase II trial is June of next year. Are there any questions?" Silence. After three seconds, Chad asked, "Are the functions still okay with that date?" Still there was no answer, just the clicking of cell phone keys. People were obviously very busy. "Okay, then. Let's move on."

Mike sat back in shock. June of next year? That was 12 months from today. What could possibly take so long?

Though Chad barely got through all the slides, the meeting finished on time, because people had to go to lunches and other meetings. Some people had actually left early while the presentation was still going on. Somehow, Mike felt that the meeting had been far too short to do any good, and far too long for the actual content it provided.

And Supragrel, even on schedule, was going to be six months too late for Timmy.

The one benefit Mike could see from the meeting, aside from getting a better sense of exactly how much faster they would have to be in order to get Supragrel to trials in time to help his son, was that he'd found that Bob was pretty good company. They headed out to lunch as soon as the meeting was over. Frankly, Mike was so annoyed by the wasted time and so worried about the timeline that he just needed to get out of the building for a while.

"So, okay. No talking. They're going to send me the slides in email. People coming in late and leaving early . . . It looks like that's a meeting I can skip from now on, right?"

"Are you kidding me, Mike? That's the key meeting of the week. You have to be there. And the silence just means that everyone's on track for their milestones. No need to talk about it if there aren't any changes."

Mike was all but certain he knew what the problem was: those milestones that everyone spent so much time thinking about. He'd seen the problem before. But he had to get Altus Labs to see it for themselves . . . starting right now, with Bob.

"All right, so the meeting's important and I've got to go. But, what's the deal with these milestones? Why is everyone so focused on them here at Altus?"

"Basically, we run the entire company like a train schedule. We choose a date for each key milestone for each drug—let's say First Tox Dose or First Human Dose, or First Registration Dose. Senior management approves these dates. Then the functional managers take the milestone date and define mini-milestones for their teams to ensure that the teams support this goal. Everybody is held accountable for being on-time. That way we make sure we deliver on time."

"So, what happens if someone is late?"

"Don't be late. If it happens we try to figure out why, but if you're the project manager and it's your fault, or if it just happens on your watch, then you can forget your bonus for that year. So, don't be late. But, you know, it happens. When it does we just adjust the other milestones and mini-milestones accordingly and move on."

The problem with these milestones, Mike could have told him, is that they couldn't allow for the inherent uncertainty in the kind of work that Altus did. There's the uncertainty of experimental science as a whole. There are studies that sometimes need to be repeated because of unforeseen problems. And then, when you get a government bureau like the Food and Drug Administration involved, you can never tell how long they'll take to review the study design, for example. There could be any number of reasons for delays. Mike had seen plenty at Versa, and he knew Altus couldn't be much different.

Mike grinned at Bob. "You ever heard of Schedule Chicken?"

"Schedule what?"

"Schedule Chicken. We used to play it all the time back at Versa, when we were still using the milestone schedule approach. You've got two work streams operating in parallel, right? And they both know they're running late. And they both know the other work stream is running late. And nobody wants to be the guy who gives the bad news because, just like here, it's goodbye bonus if you're late. So, you try to stare down the guy running the other work stream, just like kids playing Chicken. You wait and wait and wait to see how long you can hold out. You try to force the other guy to blink first and give the bad news and get all the blame. It's pretty funny to watch.

"But when you're in charge it drives you crazy. Instead of giving you the bad news right when they get it and when there might be time to address the problem by maybe borrowing some people from another project, your crew waits around and everything gets later and later and more and more expensive. I'd bet you anything that you guys play a lot of Schedule Chicken at Altus, right?"

Bob laughed and just spread his hands helplessly. "That's a perfect name for it. I won a game of it last month, now that you mention it. You don't stay at Altus for 25 years without becoming a grand master."

"I bet I could tell you a little about how milestone dates work here, too. I want to hear it from you, though."

"We have standardized project plans—so-called templates—for our projects. They are well-established. Most drug development follows a reasonably similar pattern. But even with templates there are all kinds of negotiations about the date. The teams come forward with a projected milestone date. That's reviewed by either the early-stage or late-stage portfolio committee. They almost always move the suggested timeline up a little. So they'll routinely take a few months or even quarters off the suggested milestone date. Then the project manager has to figure out how to get it done regardless."

Mike smiled again. "Sure, but since you all know this is going to happen, here's what you do, right? You put a little extra time in so that the committees have something to cut. When they cut that amount, you're just fine. When they cut a little more, you have to hustle or play a little Schedule Chicken. But sometimes you get lucky and they cut less. And then you win the game right there. And everybody knows they're playing and nobody talks about it, right?"

"Yeah, you've got me again. And we do the same thing with the mini-milestones. We ask a lot of our people. So, usually the folks in the functions are assigned to a bunch of projects, five to seven at a time and sometimes more. We've got a lot of stuff to move through the pipeline. So the functional managers set mini-milestones based on the templates we have developed over time. Normally, each mini-milestone should be reachable without a problem. To allow for all the time we lose from the multitasking and switching of priorities we just add more padding to our templates. Then they cut and, well, I guess if they cut enough we're back to Schedule Chicken."

"And if they don't cut you to the bone and you end up with a little extra time, I bet nothing ever comes in early, because when something looks like it will get done early there's always something else to distract from it that might be late. Some people call it Student Syndrome, because students always seem to want to wait until the last minute and then scramble to put their stuff together." Mike felt a little sick. Schedule Chicken and all the rest were pretty funny in theory, but when a company was playing games like that with a drug that could save your son's life it was pretty hard to see the humor in it.

Bob pointed to an older man a few tables over, adjusting his thick glasses. "See that guy? He's one of our doctors. One of the best. Rumor has it that he's got about two thousand emails just sitting in his in-box. Some folks here are so busy that they sometimes skip Christmas and stay in the office until someone from HR catches them. Then they go home and work from there."

"Is everyone that far under water?"

"No, not everyone. And for sure nobody wants to be in that position. We push and push for more time, but sometimes I wonder whether you can have enough time."

The conversation drifted to other topics, but Mike had a little trouble focusing. Talking to Bob had been disturbing. People at Altus Labs were operating on negotiated timelines set and approved by top executives. Middle management broke these major milestones down into mini-milestones. Along the way there was massive protection for everyone, whether they needed it or not. There were no real incentives to finish early. The best case in this milestone system was that deliverables came in on time. But what happened when something unforeseeable happened? Well, even if most of the mini-milestones were on time most projects would be late, because there was always that one problem that pushed things out. All the padding was used up. The irony in this world was that most people met their commitments individually but a significant number of projects were late. No wonder it was going to take a year to get Supragrel ready for Phase II. That was the safest date that all this top-down, bottom-up negotiation, all this padding and protection, could result in. Mike had a lot of work ahead of him.

〰〰

Sally called that night to say she'd talked with Dr. Hart and gotten the update on Tim's surgery. She was obviously trying to hide the concern in her voice from Mike and from Tim, who was playing a computer game nearby.

"I was at the hospital today, honey, and I saw some other kids who'd just had surgeries like Tim's. They looked so exhausted, and so vulnerable, and so sick. It broke my heart, and I can't bear to think of Tim like that. Has Altus got anything for him?"

"Not yet. But the surgery and radiation are going to buy us six months of time. That doesn't work with their current timeline for Supragrel, but I think I might be able to speed them up. You know I'm going to try, baby. But for now, Dr. Hart's plan is the only strategy we have. Let me see what I can do. Okay?"

Sally was crying silently. Mike could hear her trying to suppress her tears. "I know. Believe me, I know. I wish I could work on this from over there, so I could at least be around for you and Tim, but . . . you know how it is. Hey, put him on the phone, will you?"

Mike felt himself relax a little as Tim came on the phone and they chatted about soccer practice, school, what Mike was doing over at Altus, and exactly how many new computer games a kid who was having brain surgery could expect to get. He didn't know, yet, how fast Altus could go, but he knew he was about to find out.

Chapter 4

MORE BAD NEWS

*M*ike turned around, hot cup of cappuccino carefully balanced away from his phone and his tie, and saw that Charlene had already beaten him there. She sat comfortably in one of the armchairs at the company Starbucks in Building One. From the looks of things, she'd stopped at the drycleaner in the lobby on her way. Mike wouldn't be surprised if she'd also hit the bank and stopped by the concierge service center to get some lunch or dinner reservations made. Charlene was a little like him. She hit the ground running in the morning.

She tilted her tall cappuccino toward him in a mock toast. "How's it going?"

"I'm actually pretty impressed. I can't get over how great the place looks, but you guys have also stocked it with some really good people. They're dedicated and professional. I think I'm really going to enjoy working with them."

Charlene leaned forward, grinned up at Mike and said, "But . . . "

"Yeah, okay, you're right. But . . . I'm worried because it seems to me that you leave a lot of time on the table at the end of every project. It's so inefficient and it's so easy to spot that it almost seems like it's happening on purpose."

Her grin faded. She looked over at him with a wary expression. "Better explain that, please."

"Well, I have a pretty good picture of how you run your project timelines. You have these milestones for any project. They're negotiated dates—very safe, very conservative, because it counts against people if they don't make them, regardless of why. So, everyone makes sure that there is plenty of protection for their individual tasks. There's so much padding no one needs to push, and no one's ever early."

"I know it looks that way, but I've been in project management for a long time. Maybe there are some things you haven't thought about. Some delays we can't control. Don't forget that the research and development process is inherently complex and risky. We need these safe estimates because a lot of things can go wrong."

"Sure, but given what I've seen already, I'm worried that accepting this excuse is what makes you leave too much on the table. The extra padding that goes into milestones is there to make sure that you basically operate like a train schedule. This sounds pretty good, initially. It would be great if everyone were on time. Then you'd deliver on schedule. Everyone wants that.

"But here's the problem. It doesn't make you any faster. If someone in a project gets a task done early, they probably don't say a word about it, because they don't want to be expected to deliver that fast all the time. No one wants to see their protection disappear. Also, since nobody's expecting anyone's work to finish early, there is no advantage in the current system even if part of a job does get finished faster. If that happens under this system, it just means that someone else will have the results of that task sitting in their in-box longer. A train that's early just waits at the station longer so it can start its next trip on time. Any gain in efficiency is lost. And that's a waste for you guys, right?"

Charlene nodded. "That makes sense. But do you really think the problem's that big?"

"Hmm . . . good question. I haven't done any numbers on this yet, but . . . How many projects meet their milestones?" Mike asked her.

"Well, we measure this religiously as you know. It's part of our performance evaluation process. I'm sure some of the other managers have warned you about that. Anyway, currently, we hit close to forty percent of our major milestone dates."

"Is that a good number for the industry? How about for the history of the company?"

"It's about average for the industry, but it's not good compared with our company's history. With all the work that's been coming down the pipeline, we've gotten worse and worse." Charlene winced, just thinking about it, and Mike nodded in sympathy. Forty percent was a bit of a disaster.

"And, how does Altus stack up against competitors at getting drugs to market? You seem like you'd track that sort of statistic."

"I do. I think you and I have the same instincts. The studies we purchase indicate that we're right in the middle of the pack. We'd like to do better, but it takes a long time to turn a big ship."

"I'm not too surprised. The way you manage projects here, you're asking for bad news. You don't encourage or reward early finishes. And if something goes wrong, because of the games your teams play with scheduling, the project is doomed to be late. Basically, if something good happens and you are ahead of time, then you don't have a way to take advantage of this early finish. And if something bad happens, if things take longer and a milestone is pushed out, it ripples through the entire project and you're late. Like a train that has a delay and can't ever catch up."

"All right." Charlene sighed and gulped the last of her coffee. "I hate hearing this, because it means I've missed stuff I should have been seeing."

Mike leaned forward. "Let's see. We are in the first week of June right now. The Supragrel team is just coming off a Phase I clinical trial, so they're at a logical point to think through the next steps. I think it's time to round them up and start the planning process. Right now they are slated to get to Phase II in June of next year. But I promise you, Charlene, I can get you there faster."

Charlene smiled. "Okay, Mike. I'm willing to let you try to make me look good. What do you need from me?"

"Just two things. I need your endorsement. Let's bring the team together and tell them you're trying something new. You're thinking about piloting a new approach to Project Management. Then I need your support in challenging the templates."

Charlene thought for a while. It wouldn't be hard to persuade the current project manager of Supragrel to give up her responsibilities. She had six other projects to monitor. As a new contractor, Mike was something of an unknown. That might make the functions a little nervous. However, it wouldn't be a bad thing to try something different, and this was exactly the sort of information Charlene had hoped he'd gather, exactly the kind of shaking up that their current planning strategies needed.

"Go ahead. You have my support. Schedule the team for a planning session and I'll be there. I'd like to monitor this closely. I can't wait to see that plan."

~~~

Mike looked around the room with satisfaction. Charlene had done an outstanding job getting the team together. She had sent out an endorsement note to all of her direct reports as well as to her peers in the functions. As a result, the initial planning meeting had better attendance that Mike could have hoped for. All the key project members for Supragrel were there: two people from clinical operations, one from pharmacokinetics, three from the medical organization, one engineer from manufacturing. Even a representative from regulatory affairs showed up. She'd also gotten a statistician and two technical writers, and persuaded the project's lead physician to come.

Charlene said all the right things when she opened the meeting. She mentioned that they were looking for new and better ways to improve project execution. She emphasized to everyone that in the coming days she and

Mike would need the full attention of everyone to help them run this experiment. She told them they were all interested in seeing if it could work at Altus. She also didn't forget to mention that the functional leaders were fully behind this effort. Everyone in the room knew that Charlene had done her homework. They knew that she always did. And they knew that if she didn't have faith in what was about to happen, she wouldn't have been in the room at all.

Mike was pleased. Charlene had gotten him off to a great start, and the friendly collegiality of the people who worked at Altus meant that there was a great working atmosphere in the room. This was important, because Mike planned to work this team hard.

He needed to understand the status quo better before pushing hard for acceleration. So, after all the introductions and pleasantries were properly handled, he opened the discussion: "I took a good long look at the project documentation and noticed that you've allocated a lot of time to get Supragrel into Phase II. The target date to enroll a first patient into a new trial is June of next year. Since I'm new to the pharmaceuticals industry, can you guys give me a look at the complexities you're expecting to deal with in that timeframe?"

Trent Harrison, the lead physician, was the first to answer. "Let me tackle this one for you, Mike. First of all there are a lot of fairly standard things that need to get done before the Phase II trial. We need to have a sound protocol that outlines the trial in all details. This is a key document that is under a lot of scrutiny by the FDA and other regulatory agencies abroad. Then, we need to get the sites that will conduct the trials ready. We need to select the sites that will actually conduct the patient treatments. So we have to train physicians in hospitals and we have to make sure that the hospitals know how to document properly and consistently what they are doing. We need to get all these sites inspected and approved. We have to develop the data-capture systems to collect the trial data systematically. Some of this is work that we'll outsource to third parties. That means contracts have to be written, budgets have to be approved, you know the kind of thing. But on top of this, Supragrel is a special case. We think it's a drug that has the potential be very effective in the treatment of high-risk brain cancers such as anaplastic astrocytomas or glioblastomas, in children in particular. Our early research indicates that Surpagrel will cause reduced side effects and offer higher efficacy. We just need to prove it.

But because Supragrel is for kids, we need to conduct a pediatric Phase II study. That means we have to clear some extra hurdles for the special regulatory requirements for pediatric studies."

Mike probed further: "Like what?"

Trent leaned forward, obviously in his element. "For us to start any study in children, we need to be certain that this drug actually works at all. So, we need to be able to show that it improves efficacy in adults. Those studies are on their way. The early results look good, but we have to finish up the data collection on these and develop a report."

Mike nodded. "Is there more?"

"Yes, we need a solid understanding of how the drug metabolizes in children. That means we need to conduct some in-depth studies to arrive at MTD," the physician replied.

"Sorry, Trent, I still don't have all the acronyms down. MTD?"

Trent chuckled. "Yeah, and we're always coming up with new ones, I know. MTD stands for maximum tolerable dose. It means we need to have a clear understanding of the safe dose and the exact formulation before we can proceed with any Phase II trials in children."

Eileen Sanders, from regulatory, jumped in. "Let's not forget that the FDA protects children in particular, since they are a much more vulnerable patient group. Hence there are a lot more regulatory hurdles to clear. We should expect a lot of scrutiny before the FDA will give us the okay to move forward."

Mike understood. Besides the purely operational side of getting this project done, there were clearly a lot of scientific and regulatory issues to deal with for this particular drug. For the rest of the day Mike asked the team to look in detail at all the remaining tasks for Supragrel. His goal was to tease out all the steps that actually had to occur prior to the start of Phase II. By reviewing existing project plan templates and the team's collective knowledge, they were able to hash out a straw man project plan on the first day. That plan gave Mike slightly better news than he had hoped for. The network of tasks for the Supragrel project that would take them from completing the Phase I trial to starting the Phase II trial was not small, but it wasn't overwhelmingly complex either. Off the top of their heads, and with the help of the templates, the group had come up with about two hundred and fifty tasks that needed to be managed over the estimated twelve-month period. Mike and Charlene sent the team home that night with the assignment to think of any work that needed to be done in this project that hadn't been accounted for yet.

That evening, Mike loaded all the tasks for Supragrel into the Critical Chain software. On Monday he would introduce the team to Critical Chain. He knew he'd have a lot of talking and explaining to do, but he had something much more important to take care of first. Timmy.

Mike's plane touched down two hours before Tim's surgery. He made it to the hospital in plenty of time to spend a few quiet minutes with Sally, and a longer time with Tim, talking about the surgery and what would happen, and what Tim's recovery would be like. He reminded Tim that he'd be there when Tim woke up, and that he'd stay for two days after that, but then he had to go back to work to try to get Tim his medicine faster. Tim nodded his understanding shakily and reminded Mike that he had promised to call or videochat every single night, so Tim could hear all about what he was up to. Mike hugged him hard and promised again.

No parent should ever have to see his child looking small and scared, wearing a hospital gown, being wheeled away into an operating room. No parent should have to wait through the long, quiet, restless hours until the surgeon can report on the outcome. And no parent should have to listen to his child's terrified whimpers as he struggles back up from anesthesia. Mike and Sally had never held each other so tightly, spoken so little, or needed each other so much.

The biopsy of the tumor cells that had been removed had confirmed Dr. Hart's worst fears. Tim had a glioblastoma with tentacles that were already stretching out through his brain. Everyone knew it was nearly always a death sentence. Everyone knew that now all they could do was to move as fast as possible to give Tim as much time as possible.

Mike and Sally alternated shifts at the hospital for that day and the next two. Waking or sleeping, Timmy always had one of them with him. The surgeon had removed a large portion of the tumor. Right now, the only goal was to help Tim recover from surgery so he would have the strength to handle the radiation and chemotherapy he needed. Sally was going to shoulder the burden of most of that care. Watching her hold their son's hand, Mike knew that she didn't think of it as a burden. It hurt horribly to know that he was going to have to leave them again, to heal up on their own, but Sally looked at him with a small smile.

"I'm glad you could get home for the surgery, sweetheart. Tim was so much braver with you here, and I don't know how I'd have gotten through all that waiting without you."

"Me too. I'd have gone crazy stuck out there in Chesterton, waiting."

Sally kissed him. "I know you can do it. I wish you could do it from here, but I know that you can't. And I know that if you're there . . . well, you aren't Superman, hon, but you do some amazing stuff. Go and be amazing. Timmy and I will take care of each other. And we'll talk to you every day."

Kissing them both, and tucking a new game cartridge under Tim's pillow for him to find later, Mike stepped out of the room, squared his shoulders, and headed back to the airport for the flight east.

Chapter 5

A NEW PLAN

*G*ood morning. Thanks for a great start to our work last week. We accomplished a lot. Over the next two days what I want us to do is to take a hard look at this project. Last week we listed two hundred and fifty tasks that need managing. Did anyone come up with any missing ones that we need to add?"

Met with silence, Mike nodded with satisfaction. "Okay then. You all know what needs to be done. You have an idea when the project needs to be completed. As it stands, the deadline is June of next year. Lives can be saved by making this medicine available earlier. So, we want to find out what's the fastest possible timeline that we can develop to get Supragrel from the completion of the ongoing work in Phase I to the start of the Phase II trial? Do we really have to wait for June next year or are there better ways? That's why we are here. I need your knowledge to help me figure this out. Are you in?" Mike heard murmurs and saw nods of assent.

In the back of the room the regulatory manager, Eileen, raised her hand. "How do we know when we have found the optimal path for this project?"

This was the question Mike had hoped for. "Well, Eileen, that's a great question. You need to understand that we're not looking for perfection. That's impossible. We're looking for something that is much better than what's been done before. Based on your work last week, we're going to go through each task and decide how closely its delivery depends on the delivery of other tasks. We also need to understand if a task is a prerequisite for other tasks in this project. What we're trying to do is to understand which tasks depend on which other tasks. Sometimes, there are tasks that are worked in series when there is no real reason for it. If we find those, we can go ahead and 'break' the link between them. If we do that whenever possible, we can save a lot of time. Okay?"

She nodded, and so did other people.

"But we can do more. We need to figure out what we call the 'touch time' for each task. What I mean by touch time is the actual time it takes to get a task done if you do only that task. When my wife wants to know how long it's going to take me to mow the lawn, I pad it a little. I usually tell her it's going to take all afternoon. I know I'm going to stand around talking with my neighbor for a while, and stop for a beer, and decide to take a break and walk to the mailbox on the corner, then check the scores on the game—you know the kind of thing I mean. But if I just mow the lawn? Ninety minutes."

There were some laughs from the group as people recognized the all-too-familiar scenario.

"You all know there's a lot of time in your conventional task estimates where things just sit around. You put in some extra time to deal with the fact that things in R&D are unpredictable. You put in a little more because you are multitasking. You put in a little more than that because you can, and because nobody wants to be late, and because we all know that management will take some away. So, I want to ask you all for something radical. I want to know what your true touch time is for a particular task. How long does it really take to get a protocol written? How long does it take when you are focusing on just writing the protocol and nothing else? In the standard template I saw a task estimate of four weeks for this task. There have been entire theses written in that timeframe. So, how long does it really take if you do everything you can to do the work with as much focus as possible? By focused I mean, when you need something, you don't shoot off an email and wait around for a response, but instead you get on the phone or walk over to someone's cube. That's the time estimate I want from you."

"But what happens if it takes longer than our esti-mate?"

"Here's the point. If you give me aggressive but doable durations, sometimes things are going to take longer than you'd predicted." He looked around the room, smiling at the expressions of shock he saw. "I know. I told you I was going to make you faster and now I'm saying you'll end up being late. And you will be, from time to time, with individual tasks. But it won't matter to the project as a whole, and you won't get penalized for it . . . unless you've just been blowing off work that is on the Critical Chain, of course. What we're going to do is to calculate a 'time buffer' to protect the overall project schedule. This buffer will allow time for execution risks. Instead of putting in our personal buffers on each task, we will create a project buffer as a shared protection for the whole team to use.

"I'll talk more about the buffer in a little while. The thing to get about it right now is that when you're using Critical Chain, no one is going to punish you if you don't hit your task estimate exactly. All you have to do is to

work with as much focus as possible on tasks that are crucial to the project."

The room was quiet. This was a new concept.

"Once we're done figuring out task durations and
which tasks depend on which other tasks, we'll apply
resources to the tasks. Then we can use this software
to compute what is called the Critical Chain. This is
the longest chain through a project network that takes
into account all task and all resource limitations. Now,
every task is important in this network, but those on the
Critical Chain have one special characteristic. They're
the ones that are most likely to slow you down. Every day
you get behind on a Critical Chain task causes the project
to come in a day later. So wouldn't it be great to find out
which tasks are on the Critical Chain?"

Trent nodded his agreement. "Sure, but when will we
be able to see this Critical Chain?"

"Excellent question. We need to get the network of
tasks right. We need to know which tasks you need to
do in what order. We need to know what resources they
need and what their touch times are. I want you all to
take a pass through all the tasks for your function today
and get those things done. If you take just a few minutes
to think about each task and go with your gut, then you'll
be done with that by tonight and I can run a first analysis.

Tomorrow morning we can look at the Critical Chain of this project for the first time."

Trent folded his arms and frowned. "Mike, it's still not clear to me how this makes us faster. Aren't you really just re-ordering the same amount of work? That can't save time."

"That's not all we're doing, though reorganization is part of it. If we do our job in this planning cycle, we can come up with a sequence of key tasks that gets us from A to B. We will also have identified the true touch time for those key tasks. As a result we'll have a strong plan that keeps our focus where it needs to be as we go into project execution. Make sense?" People nodded their heads.

"Then, we'll meet on a weekly basis. We'll discuss which tasks are on the Critical Chain. Those tasks will need to be worked with high priority. Everyone in this room will be given permission to focus on Critical Chain tasks until they are done. That way the work can be handed to the next person who is waiting for it. We'll minimize multitasking. Back at Versa we call this 'running the relay race.' Okay?" Again people nodded.

"Then, last, there's the project manager. It's my job to help overcome obstacles, run interference so that you can do your job, and screen the project network. I'll constantly look for any risks to tasks, in particular those that are on the Critical Chain. Now, the PM will need your help identifying these risks. If you find and track those early on, the team will be much better prepared. You'll most likely have a plan for dealing with them in place by the time a risk materializes. That's the last piece to the puzzle."

Trent still looked skeptical. "We are all busy, and we're used to multitasking. I've got more than Supragrel on my desk. We all do. It seems like in the company where you worked before, you were trying to minimize multitasking. But we're too busy not to multitask, aren't we? I mean, can you tell me how we're supposed to get anything done?"

"Sure. I'd be happy to." Mike cleared his throat. "Let's take a simple example—again, like the lawn-mowing thing, it's something I do all the time. I read too many books at once. Sometimes, if I look at my night stand I find I've got a teetering stack of ten or twelve books that I'm reading all at once. Now, since this is pleasure reading I'm not really interested in efficiency. But if it were critical for me to get all the reading done and do something with the content, I'd be in trouble.

"Say I have ten books to read, each with two hundred pages. If I read twenty pages per day and I multitask, I'll have read twenty pages of each book after ten days of reading. And I probably won't have a clue what's happening in any of them. After twenty days, I'll be forty pages into each book, and I'll finish them all somewhere between days ninety-one and one hundred. And since

I don't have a perfect memory, in all likelihood, I will have to go back to remind myself of what I've read. Going back over material I've already read is what I call switching costs. Switching costs in the real world can be even higher that. They can easily make up twenty to thirty percent of the whole task.

"But, if I read in a focused way, I will have read all of my first book on day ten. I will finish my second book on day twenty. At the end of day ninety I will have read nine out of ten books and be ready to start my tenth. I won't have any redundant reading to do. I won't have any switching costs.

"So, the first takeaway is: Reading in a focused way, I will have read nine out of ten books on day ninety. By multitasking I won't have completed any of the books by then. It's all still work in progress. That means I cannot fully take advantage of the content of any of the books, nor can I pass any of the books to someone else. Now, the switching costs are a big deal. The more books I read in parallel, the harder it will be to keep track of where I am. If there were a hundred books on my night stand, I would get nothing done. I would have forgotten what was in the first twenty pages of the first book by the time I finished the first twenty pages of the hundredth book. I would have to read it all over again."

Mike surveyed the room, trying to assess how well everyone was following him. "Does this help?"

It did.

The room buzzed with the sound of the team getting to work. Everybody was interested to find out what the Critical Chain for Supragrel was going to look like. Mike knew it would be a long day for the team. Getting the wiring right for two hundred and fifty tasks isn't a small job. There would have to be a lot of discussion among the clinicians, the pharmacokinetics specialist, the writers and statisticians, and others who had never spoken to each other about how they could optimize the work on their shared project.

After an intense day, the team finally finished. They were confident they had gotten the linkages right between tasks in the network, and the durations were as close to touch times as they could be. They had also created a resource model that tied tasks to the people responsible for them. By about 6 P.M. the network had been plotted out for the third time that day, and Mike had small groups of people looking over specific parts of the network. The scientists were enjoying themselves. The process was new and exciting, and discovering how to shorten the path to success felt kind of like an invention. At about 7.30 P.M., Mike sent the team home to get some sleep. The next day they would get their first look at the Critical Chain.

~~~

Mike had asked everybody to come back at 7 A.M. Because he didn't want to torment them more than necessary, breakfast had already arrived as they began to fill the room. Everyone heaped plates with fruit salad and filled coffee cups. While they waited for the pancake guy Mike had brought in to start flipping hotcakes off the griddle, they chatted about the weather, their plans for their summer vacation, and how little sleep they'd had last night. Here and there Mike could hear some jokes about Critical Chain. Trent pretended to be enormously relieved that someone was finally here to tell him why his projects were always late. Eileen commented that she was hoping to get Mike to do a Critical Chain analysis on why her boyfriend was never on time for a date. It was all well-meaning, and as Mike hooked his laptop to the overhead he was glad to hear everyone so cheerful this early in the morning. He knew he'd convince any doubters today.

"Okay, ladies and gentlemen. You are two-thirds done. Yesterday you got the wiring right. We made great progress putting in focused durations. So I've loaded the updated project schedule into the Critical Chain project management software. I'll calculate the Critical Chain for this project and then see how we can optimize the project further. This is the key objective for today. Depending on what kind of progress we make, we might even be done with the whole planning exercise today. How does that sound?"

That sounded very good to everyone in the room. While people had been very supportive of the process, they felt they had to get back to their "real" jobs soon. But they were intrigued. And the pancakes were really good.

Mike pressed the button to calculate the Critical Chain for Supragrel. It took about thirty seconds for the laptop to complete the calculation. The first result was surprisingly good. The Critical Chain for getting Supragrel to Stage II was about six months long and consisted of about thirty-five tasks.

Mike loved this moment. No matter how often he did it, it never got old. "Ladies and gentlemen . . . the Critical Chain for Supragrel." He hit the key to publish his laptop screen on the projector. Heads turned as everyone finally got a look at the thing they'd been talking about for days. At first, Mike knew, all they would be able to make out was a bunch of boxes symbolizing tasks and an endpoint showing December 31, only six months away.

Trent was the first to speak up. "So, Mike, are you saying that we're going to be able to deliver Supragrel within six months? We've never been that fast for something like this."

"Well, yes and no. The Critical Chain that you see here is the longest chain of tasks through the project network. In other words, if you get these tasks done in the timeframe you stated and manage all other non-critical tasks so they don't interfere with the Critical Chain, then you will be done in six months. But I also asked you to give me aggressive estimates for each task. Let's assume that this network I've got up here is as aggressive as it can be. Chances are that we will face some slippages along the way. That's why in Critical Chain project management we have the 'project buffer' I talked about yesterday: time to protect the project."

There was silence in the room. Mike could feel his team listening.

"The typical project buffer is about 50% of the Critical Chain length. So, for Supragrel, we would add three months to the project schedule. When you go out and talk about this project to senior management, you'll commit to the buffered project duration. Remember, you took all the padding out of the tasks. By creating a buffer, you get some of that padding back. But instead of managing that buffer on a per-task level, it's aggregated to the project level. That way you account for the risk that is inherent to your work. Also, you account for the fact that, no matter how amazing you are, you're not going to be perfect at executing this project plan. But you also leave room for good things to happen. If you finish right on-time or early, that means someone else can dip into the buffer if they need it."

"Nine months is pretty good," said another team member. "So we're done?"

"Well, we could stop here. But let's make sure that we have captured all possibilities to bring the schedule in. We need to take a closer look. Are all of these tasks on the Critical Chain really essential ones? Take a look at the linkages again. If there is a dependency that we can break between two tasks on the critical chain, let's break it. If we can do something in less time, then let's plug in those more aggressive estimates."

People in the room stared at the screen for a while. From the back of the room, someone from manufacturing called out: "Hey, wait! Some of my stuff is on the Critical Chain. But I've got production slots open now. If I can get the go-ahead to produce the required materials for Phase II in the next three weeks, I can get that done and have it ready for the project. You could take these tasks off the Critical Chain entirely."

"You're saying you could start to manufacture right away? Is that pricey?"

The engineer said, "Nah, it's not such a big deal. I have these slots open anyway. I just need to find someone to approve it."

"Wait a minute." Eileen chimed in. "Are we ready to commit to that? I don't think we have the regulatory approval for the dosage yet. "

People looked at Trent.

Trent thought for a second and then replied, "We don't have approval for the dosage, but the formulation of the drug isn't a problem. I think my colleague from PK will confirm that the formulation is stable. Now, we do have to get the dose approved by the FDA. However, our plan was all along to produce pills with a very low dose to begin with. In our notes to the physicians in the field we will recommend dosing a certain number of pills per day, based on different factors including body weight. Given that, we can go ahead with the manufacturing process if there is an opportunity to use an open manufacturing slot."

Eileen spoke up one more time. "But we don't have the regulatory approval yet."

Trent lost a little of his composure. "Eileen, you're not listening. As I said, we can adjust the dose by prescribing a different number of low-dose pills in a given time interval. If the FDA doesn't approve this protocol including the minimum dosage per pill, we have much bigger problems. Problems that probably mean scrapping the drug and starting over. So, why don't we just see how much time we can save by making the low-dose pills in advance and having them ready to go when we *do* get approval?"

Mike rewired the network, taking the manufacturing tasks off the Critical Chain. He reran the calculation and nodded with satisfaction. "This decision would save about four weeks.

Trent shot a smug glance in Eileen's direction. "Sounds worth it to me. Let's do it!"

Mike looked around the room. "Everybody on board with this?" He saw people nodding. "Is there more?"

The group stared at the screen. Mike knew that while they were looking for other possible breakthroughs, they were also still processing what they'd just seen—a month of time saved without anyone doing anything except thinking a little more creatively.

Then someone from the medical function said, "One issue for me is getting my protocol review meeting scheduled and then getting management focused on the job. Right now that's set to take up three weeks in the schedule. But this could be dealt with in one or two business days if the executives are on board. So if I can get someone to apply a little pressure to get the governance committee to make decisions in time, I could take this task down to two business days."

Mike rapidly made the changes, saying, "Okay, let's assume you get protocol review to approval in one week, taking into account one set of revisions. That would save you two more weeks on the Critical Chain. Who do you need to make this work?"

"Well, Mike, I guess you need to talk to Charlene. She's the one who can wrangle the top guys."

Mike understood. "Okay. Let me look into this one. For now, let's assume that we can do this."

Rerunning the software showed an additional two-week reduction of the Critical Chain. People were impressed, but Mike was not ready to stop yet. He pushed them again. "Is there more?"

The head of clinical operation raised her hand. "Well, I just talked to my assistant. We could ship samples from the Phase I studies overnight and save almost two weeks of transit time. It's a bit more money than standard shipping, but we can do it, if it's going to save us some real time."

"Okay. Let me look at the effect of these suggestions." Mike typed in the changes quickly. He hit the calculate button for the Critical Chain again. Mike smiled. He had his answer. And it was starting to look like Tim might just have his, too. He called for more ideas, but this time there were no further suggestions.

"So, what this tells us is the following. If we incorporate all the suggested modifications, we can reach First Patient Visit in Phase II in four months with no buffer. This time, even with a fifty percent buffer, we will be able to reach this milestone by December 31."

Trent spoke up as usual. "This seems doable, but let me say that I'm also pretty nervous over here. If I look at the Critical Chain as it is, a lot of things need to fall in line perfectly. Plus, there are lot of tasks on the Critical Chain that have to do with obtaining regulatory approval. That's something we hardly have any influence over. You can't make the government go faster. Are you sure we want to give these dates to management? I mean, what if we miss this date?"

Mike knew he had to address this issue. If people were worried they would be evaluated based only on their milestone dates, then that was where their focus would be. They'd never follow the methodology and learn to run the relay race.

"Well, we are here to find out how we can move this project faster. We have squeezed this plan until its hurts so we can optimally organize all the activities that are in our control. We have arranged those activities so we can use the fastest ways to get the work done. That is terrific. But I know it's nerve-wracking, especially since you've always been evaluated on hitting deadlines before, and I'm trying to convince you that this is not going to happen this time. And that's hard to believe. Let me take it up with Charlene, and see if I can get you guys some more formal reassurance.

"Ultimately, though, if we are able to come in any faster than the original date, then nobody in this room should have anything to worry about. So, let me ask all of you this question: Is there anything in this network that doesn't sound realistic? Is there any assumption that we're making, implicitly or explicitly, that doesn't make sense?"

Trent, naturally, chipped in. "You didn't really address my concerns about multitasking before. If we end up adopting this new timeline, what do we do if we have conflicts with other responsibilities to other projects?"

That was indeed a risk. Mike had permission to run this experiment. Charlene had lined up the support of her peers. But how strong would that support really be during execution? If Altus took Critical Chain any further, they would install a process to establish better priorities. But it was not time for that yet.

"You're right. This is something you might not get perfect right away. But if Altus does adopt this timeline and if you know your task is on the Critical Chain, then please work on it in as focused a way as possible. Once you're done, hand your work to the next person and get back to the stuff you've had to put to the side. If there are conflicts you just can't get out of with other assignments, then please let me know. I'll work hard to get those resolved. Does this sound fair?"

It did.

With that concern addressed, if not completely resolved, the team was done. Mike was pleased to be able to give everybody a half day back, hoping they would take it as evidence that working in a focused and efficient manner could have some tangible rewards. While they walked back to their cubes, expressing excitement, interest, and a little doubt about the new timeline, Mike went back to his desk. He needed to review the project schedule one more time to understand all critical handoffs. That's where teams mess up and lose time, and he couldn't let that happen. He also needed to talk to Charlene. He had some great news for her about Supragrel.

Chapter 6

CROSSING
THE RUBICON

*T*he Starbucks at Altus was where people got some of their most important work done. Mike and Charlene used it for fairly regular meetings, and met up accidentally there every now and again as well. This time, since the meeting was an important one, Mike had prepared a little chart for her, to sum up the results of the network building session.

When he arrived, Charlene was already sipping her latte while punching quick email replies on her phone. His cappuccino—extra shot, extra dry—was waiting for him.

"How's it going Mike? How was the meeting?"

"It was interesting. I think you'll be pleased. You remember your original plan, right? The idea was to start the Phase II trial in June of next year. We went over the details of the project plan and zeroed in on all the cross-functional handoffs that have to take place. We also took a hard look at some of the real durations for some of the tasks. That saved about three months, even including a buffer. Our initial new schedule was six months with a buffer of three months. That buffer will provide us with good insurance."

"Yeah. I get that. Mike, nine months? That's great. That's a lot of improvement for a few days of planning."

"It is, but that's not all. There are three key points that would allow you to be even faster. We'll need your help for those, though."

"Faster? Okay, now I'm really interested."

"The first thing has to do with manufacturing the materials. We have manufacturing slots available now and we could start the process of making the drugs for the Phase II trial immediately. You could save about a month on the schedule with that change alone."

"Did manufacturing agree to do that?"

"Well, it was their idea. They just need you and their Director to approve it."

"That shouldn't be a problem. We have done it from time to time, but we've never really figured out how much time it can save. What else?"

"The second place where you can save some real time is with the Protocol Review Meeting. Right now, it's estimated to be a three-week process. Most of that is just waiting for the review committee to get ready for the review. They could actually do this in one week or less. All we need is the buy-in of the review committee to agree to read the documents and hold its approval meeting as soon as the documents are ready."

Charlene looked uncomfortable, which was understandable. Nobody wants to be the one who has to tell upper management to get in gear. "Well, it's not all that easy to get everyone together. Are you sure that this is crucial to the timing of the project?"

"I am. The decision process is right on the Critical Chain. Any day you wait for them to meet is a day you lose on the project. It would be a shame to lose time that way, if everyone else is busting their butts to get things out the door faster."

"But how much will it save, really?"

"About two weeks, plus some buffer."

She sighed with resignation. Clearly, it was going to have to be done. Just as clearly, it was going to be a headache. "Let me work on that. It won't cost us anything. And it's not really asking people for anything other than, you know, doing their jobs. I'll need your explanation in an email, though, so that I can send it to my colleagues. Since I'm on the review committee, I should be able to make the case. What's the third thing?"

"Oh, this one you don't have to help on. The folks from clinical will just change their process slightly. They will ship the samples from the Phase I studies overnight and analyze them as they come in. It costs a bit more, and it requires a bit more overhead, but we will gain another two weeks as a result."

"So, four weeks . . . two weeks . . . another two weeks . . . If we do all this, where do we end up?"

"Well, the initial new schedule was six months with a three-month buffer. If we build in all the savings we found, then the final schedule will be four months long with a two-month buffer. In other words, you could pretty safely get Supragrel into Phase II by Christmas of this year."

"That's phenomenal. Well, it's phenomenal if we can do it. Is the team behind the new timeline?"

"It looks that way. They're a great group, and they're already starting to work together and think about faster processes. I think this is doable. They are a little worried that their performance evaluations might ride on the success of this one project. Even if we pull this in just a little bit faster than the original plan, we have to give them credit."

"Agreed. Let me take care of that. Six months. That's amazing. You realize that any day we can save on this project means a million dollars for the company in the long run? If we can pull this off or even come close, then none of the performance evaluations will be an issue. Look, I've talked to the governance committee about you, Mike. I think it's in our mutual interest that you come on board permanently as the project manager for Supragrel."

"You know, Charlene, I've been waiting for you to ask me that. I'm in."

Twenty-four hours later, all the formal approvals were in and Charlene was able to officially hire Mike as a Project Manager. After a quick conversation with HR the next morning, Mike had a new job, tons of perks he'd never use, and a fifty percent pay cut. Mike didn't care. He also had a reservation for a flight back to California. There were a few really unpleasant conversations waiting for him back at Versa—conversations he really had to have face-to-face.

〰

Mike had never minded giving notice to the companies he worked for. Business is business. Everyone moves around, and everyone knows it. But giving notice to Dan was going to be different. He'd been a boss and a mentor and a friend for years now. He deserved better than a Senior Director who'd jump ship with two weeks' notice. And he certainly deserved better than a formal letter left on his desk. Mike was going to have to go in and take the heat personally.

Dan sometimes played the wild man in the office to wake people up and get things done. Mike had seen him toss a chair across a conference room once. And the junior staff circulated the totally untrue, but very useful rumor that Dan had once set fire to a particularly unsatisfactory year-end report. But Dan wasn't faking now.

"You're doing what? You are leaving the company to join one of these pill makers? You can't be serious. What is wrong with you? This has gotta be a mid-life crisis thing. Why don't you just buy a Harley or have an affair like everyone else?"

"Look, Dan. I have a chance to make a real difference and . . . "

"Can it, Mike. I've known you for ten years now. I know when you are trying to BS me. I want to know what the story is. You are not moving across the country to work for a pill maker just because you have discovered your inner Samaritan. Tell me what the story is! Where are you really going? Who the hell bought you?"

If anyone had earned the right to hear the truth from Mike, it was Dan. He needed to know that Mike wasn't leaving Versa out of some sudden restless impulse. "Dan, Tim's got brain cancer. He's dying. There's exactly one drug that might help him, and Altus is trying to get it ready for clinical trials. But they're going to be too slow. Without me, they're going to be too slow."

Dan's anger melted into nothing. "You are not making this up, are you? This is unbelievable news. You and Sally must be terrified. I can't even imagine."

"I wouldn't leave for anything less important. But for my son . . . You know how it is."

"I'm going to do what I can for you. I'm going to get you out of your contract with us in one piece and get you the best package I can for severance. But you've got to understand that you're not going to be able to come back to Versa when . . . when it's over. I get why you're doing it. Hell, I'd do the same thing. But this is a career killer."

Mike nodded silently and offered his hand. He turned to go and heard the door to Dan's office close. It sounded shockingly final.

That was the hardest part of the day. It was merely infuriating a few hours later when Mike got the traditional "don't let the door hit you on the way out" phone call from Vincent Louis, the Senior Vice-President of HR at Versa. Vincent didn't waste any time on friendliness, or even politeness. He just demanded the return of the company laptop, which Mike had already left on his former desk for IT to pick up. He questioned Mike closely about any papers he might have at home, though everyone at Versa knew Mike had gone paperless two years ago. A check with four months of severance pay and four weeks of vacation pay would be in the mail, with an additional cash bonus that came to six months of his former salary—assuming he agreed to sign the usual waivers and non-compete agreements.

Dan had obviously kept Tim's medical condition in mind when arguing for this severance package, and Mike would have to be a fool not to sign, since Timmy's treatment and the two households he would be paying for now were already weighing on his mind. Vince reminded him how good the package was and told him to sign it as soon as the courier showed up with it, and to have it back to Versa by tomorrow unless he wanted the deal to disappear. And then he hung up, without so much as a goodbye or good luck.

At Versa's spring golf tournament last year, Vince had hugged Mike for birdying the last hole. They'd gone out for drinks after work a time or two. They sent cards at Christmas. And that severance phone call had taken less than five minutes. No question about it, Mike's career at Versa was over.

He signed Versa's non-compete agreement, the settlement offer, and Altus Labs' official offer letter. But he paused, just for a second, before he did. He finally really got what people meant when they say they had crossed the Rubicon. He'd done it today. The die had been cast.

Chapter 7

THE TOWN HALL MEETING

*T*he next Monday morning meeting was a little more exciting than the first one Mike had attended. Charlene had shocked the room when she announced that the Supragrel milestone date would be moving from June of next year to December 31 of this year. No one had ever seen such an extreme change before, certainly not such an extreme change in such a good direction! Bob told Mike that nothing like it had ever happened in the twenty-five years he'd been at Altus, and he'd never heard of it happening even before then. Previously, if there had been a change in the milestone date, it was because of a delay. In fact, during the morning meeting someone asked her, twice, to confirm that she was moving the milestone six months earlier, not six months later. She confirmed it, masking a smile. Then, she mentioned that she'd hired Mike to captain the Supragrel project and told them that the Supragrel team would go into more detail at the town hall meeting scheduled for Wednesday of that week. She'd done a perfect job setting the stage.

These monthly town hall meetings took place in the auditorium at Altus. Set up like a movie theater, with a stage up front, theater seating, plenty of room in the back for eavesdroppers, and with the ability to videostream the event to the desks of those who couldn't make it to the meeting, the auditorium was the perfect place for big, dramatic announcements.

The meeting was scheduled for 10 A.M. By 9:45 A.M. that Wednesday the room was already three-quarters full. Mike looked around and greeted people he knew and made polite talk with those he didn't while he took his seat in the front. This would be his official introduction to Altus, and he was riding high on adrenaline and, truth be told, a little bit of nerves. Charlene took the stage shortly after Mike sat down. As usual, she was dressed to kill in a sharp, navy blue suit, take-charge heels, and a pearl necklace. With no hesitation she stepped to the microphone and started the meeting the moment the hands of the clock hit ten.

"Good morning! Wow, what fantastic attendance. I guess I got your attention on Monday, hmm? I'm sure that most of you are here today to learn what the story is behind the announcement we made then, that we'd be moving the milestone of one of our cancer drugs six months earlier than expected. Believe me, I am aware that this is unusual. So I want to explain what's going on.

"I've been with Altus for fifteen years now, and in that time I have seen us push out milestones for various reasons. Sometimes the FDA has requested additional time to review documents; sometimes we've needed to respond to bad scientific data; sometimes there's simply too much work. Everybody here is working harder than ever before. But our project durations are getting longer and longer. This is a disservice to our company stakeholders, but most importantly it's a disservice to our patients. Every day that a project is late is another lost day before we can ship the drug to the market. It is another lost day before we can get the drug into the hands of a doctor and ultimately another lost day before we can help our patients.

"For all these good reasons we are piloting a new project management methodology called Critical Chain. We believe it will allow us to become faster and more nimble. This methodology relies on three simple principles:

One: Aggressive but Realistic Schedules—Create the best possible schedule to get a project from where we are to where we want to go, taking into account the inevi-table bumps in the road.

Two: Running the Relay Race—Apply focus on key tasks that are drivers of the overall timeline. Get those tasks done quickly and move the results of the work quickly to the next person. Have the mindset of a relay racer.

Three: Proactive Risk Management—Identify and address as early as possible all key risks that might impact the project and its timeline negatively.

"We have decided to use Supragrel as a test case for this new system. We've already had the first planning meeting where we focused on time-optimized schedules. Out of that meeting came the improvements in our sched-uling that made us confident we can move our commit-ment significantly earlier. But we know this can't happen all by itself. We need your help to make it more than just a schedule change. We need your help to make it a reality.

"We have a new project manager on board who has quite a bit of experience with this methodology. He came to us from a semiconductor company that has been using this approach for a number of years. I've asked Mike to speak to us this morning about his experience with Critical Chain and also about his personal background. You've probably already met him, but please take a minute to welcome Mike Knight."

There was warm applause as Mike stood, shook Charlene's hand, and took the microphone. He smiled at the group.

"Thanks for coming. I'm really pleased to see so many of you here. As Charlene has indicated, I've just been around Altus for a little while. In that time, I've been impressed by the scientific depth of this organization and by the dedication of every person I've met here.

"I was hired to find ways to accelerate our drug development process. In my previous company we had similar challenges—unpredictable research and development, bureaucratic structures, technical challenges—and we overcame them. The question is, can the same principles apply here at Altus? I believe they can. To prove it—to you, to our bosses, and to ourselves—we've picked a project that could see enormous, almost instantaneous benefits from an improved project planning and execution process. This project is Supragrel.

"Over a period of three days we built a schedule, and then asked the Supragrel team a series of key questions. The first set of questions was about why tasks are done in a particular order. We asked the group to consider, for each task: Is this task really necessary to start the next one in line? Can this task be worked in parallel with any other task, or can it at least overlap? These are simple questions, but getting good answers to them can require some creative thinking. We found quite a few examples where we actually could "break" the link between two tasks and conduct the work on several tasks in parallel. We learned a lot about how the functions can work together more effectively when they really understand how they depend on each other. These are some of the most important ways we can speed up a timeline.

"The second set of questions we asked them to consider involved how long it really takes to get a task done. These are the really hard questions, because no one wants to admit how fast they could be working, compared to how fast they actually are. And we were not interested in safe estimates. No, we wanted to know how long you actually work on something. We're talking about the difference between 'I can get this document to you by close of business on Friday of next week' vs. 'I just need four uninterrupted hours to write the damned thing.' For obvious reasons, asking this question and getting good answers is another way to speed up our timeline.

"The third set of questions had to do with the resources required for each task. Without resource information, you can't be sure team members aren't overbooked, so you can't trust the time estimates in the schedule. Of course, you can't put in every resource for every task, but you can do enough to make a credible picture.

"Once we have the answers to these questions we can find the best way to get a project done as quickly as possible. The Supragrel team did a phenomenal job with this planning session. Some of you already know this. We went into that meeting thinking that the next milestone date, which is starting the Phase II clinical trial, would be summer of next year. However, the team feels that, using Critical Chain, we can deliver this portion of the project by the end of this year—which means six months of savings. Saving time and money and maybe even some lives. I think they deserve some applause for that."

Naturally, the team got the applause that Mike called for. He was fairly certain, though, that there were a lot of nervous people in the audience, trying to figure out how Supragrel's increased speed would affect their pet projects. Were they all going to have to crank out that kind of result? Why mess with the way it had always worked before?

"So, we've got the new milestone date. We've got the new timeline. We've got the new system. All we need to do is make it happen. Fortunately . . ." Mike nodded over at the group of doctors sitting together in the front of the auditorium, "While for some of you, this actually *is* brain surgery, for the rest of us it's not rocket science. With the help of Critical Chain software we will be able to identify which tasks are the most critical ones each week. We will be able to track which tasks drive the timeline. What that means for you is that if a task you are working on is a Critical Chain task, any day it's late is a day that the project will be late. The one key behavior that I need from anyone who is involved in Supragrel is this: If your task is on the Critical Chain, focus on it. Treat it like it's your only task until it's done. Minimize multitasking. Get this work completed, and hand over the results of your work to the next person waiting for it. If we all do this, the project will work like a gigantic relay race. And like runners in a relay we will each be trying to finish our lap as soon as we can, so the whole team can get to the finish line as quickly as possible.

"We know the timing on Supragrel is tight. We know that when you plan this aggressively, something unexpected always happens to slow things down. It's just the nature of the beast. But we're doing something new here. You're not going to be penalized for being late if it's for a reason like that. We know that unexpected stuff happens. You can have the best family budget in the world, but then the fridge breaks, one of the kids breaks a window at the neighbor's house, or you have a little more fun on vacation that you can exactly afford. For times like that, we've all got an emergency fund set aside. We'll do the same here with our timeline.

"You've all seen how incredible the new schedule looks. If all of our best-case assumptions come true, we could be done as early as Halloween. But, you know, if all my best-case assumptions came true, I'd be cashing in a lottery ticket at the end of every week. So, since we know life isn't perfect, we have a buffer as our emergency fund for this project. Instead of money, our buffer banks time. It's holding two months for us right now, and we'll only take time out of it when a Critical Chain task is in real trouble.

"We're going to make it very easy to track how our race is going. Every week we'll update how far along each task is. Based on the input of each team member, we'll be able to calculate something called a fever chart. A fever chart shows us how much work we have done, how much we have left to do, as well as how much of our buffer we've used up and how much is left. This is what a typical fever chart might look like. On the x-axis it shows us the percent of the Critical Chain we have completed. On the y-axis it shows how much buffer time we have used up. The colors show how much trouble we're in: the more buffer is used, the hotter the fever. Green means the project is on track for an early finish. Yellow means the project is on track for an on-time finish, but the team needs to watch out for additional buffer consumption. Red means: Watch out; if the team doesn't find ways to gain back some of the time, it will be late. Being in the red does not mean that everything is lost. It just means that the team needs to execute a buffer recovery plan."

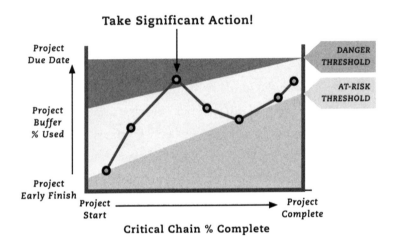

Figure 1: Fever Chart

Mike pointed at the lower-right corner of the chart. "There's virtually no way that we're going to be here at our finish, because that would mean we had used up none of our buffer." He pointed toward the top right of the chart. "And it's almost certain that we'll come in by this point. But even if we use up every hour of buffer, we're going to finish six months before the original milestone. And we can do that.

"At least we can do that if we can really focus on key tasks as soon as they're ready for us. I know the Supragrel team is committed to that. My job as the Project Manager of this project is to help make that happen by looking ahead and identifying any potential risks to the plan. To do that, I'll be asking for a lot of input. If you can think of an execution risk for us, share it. We want to know what we don't know yet.

"That's all there is to it. If we do this right, then we will be done by Christmas, maybe even as early as Halloween. I'm betting you have some questions. So, let me have it."

Mike loved Q&A. There were always some easily anticipated questions that he had well-prepared answers to. But someone always threw something in from way out in left field. The first question was one of the easy ones: "Has this approach been successful elsewhere, and what are the major obstacles that could keep us from getting it right?"

"I'm glad you asked that. This approach has worked well in the semiconductor industry, aerospace and defense, and in manufacturing. In my previous company we used it for a number of years to get our commitments stabilized and to accelerate the time it took us to get products developed. Now, to make it work, you need a few crucial things to fall into place. At the project level the most important part is to build a credible plan and then have a thorough week-to-week updating process. If we all look at the same things, and we all understand the priorities of what needs to get done each week, it's going to work. Of course, there will be things that are out of our control. There's the FDA; there's unreliable or inexplicable scientific data; there are changes that management makes and forgets to tell us about. Those are out of the control of the project team. But now we have a way to communicate clearly about that kind of problem. Maybe we can solve them ourselves. Maybe we need to get senior management in to fix them. But if we can see them, we can deal with them."

One of the stats guys stood up and asked, "If it's so effective, why doesn't everyone use this Critical Chain stuff?" Mike had heard this question a lot over the years. He always took it as a good sign when people asked, figuring it meant they were on the way to being convinced.

"I'm with you. I think everyone should. But life's not perfect, right? Why isn't everyone buff? Why doesn't everyone give up drinking, smoking, and gambling? The basics of Critical Chain are simple, but they require discipline and focus. If we have a time-sensitive task to do, then we need to work on it with as much focus as possible until it's done. And every minute there are hundreds of distractions in our way. There is the meeting we have to go to. There is the chit-chat about the Monday night football game at the water cooler. There are bosses who want to talk about their latest ideas. There's email. Phone calls. A little disagreement with your significant other. Anything. It takes real work to keep those distractions off your back and focus on the one thing that matters most."

Charlene asked the group for one more question to wrap up the session. That's when the left-field question got lobbed in. "We all know what you did before you came here. We all know this was, pretty much, a demotion for you. Why did you take this job, anyway?"

Mike gave Charlene a quick glance. Charlene stood up and said, "This is a great question. I'll let Mike answer it, but before he does let me say that Mike is a very unusual case, and before hiring him the Altus management team had to consider the ramifications deeply. After a careful review, we all agreed that he is a terrific fit. Mike?"

Mike took a deep breath, and went for it. "My eight-year-old son has brain cancer. It's a kind that won't respond to conventional treatment. Supragrel is a drug that might be able to help him, and help a lot of other kids like him. So when I heard about it and about Altus, I thought that the only thing I could do to save my son is to try to help all of you work better and smarter and faster. I can't make the drug, or run the trials, or treat the patients. But I can help all of the people who do all of this work be more efficient. It's not just my son, though. There are a lot of people waiting for this drug. Even if we do get Supragrel out on time, it might not save my son. I know that. But maybe it can save him. And if it can't, maybe it can save another kid. I just feel like it's worth a try."

It was very quiet for a long, long moment. And then the sound of applause carried Mike from the stage.

~~~

Back at his desk, after taking a few minutes to pull himself together and a few more to answer several questions from people wanting to know more about Timmy, his prognosis, and his timeline, Mike took some time to call home. Tim had been on radiation treatments for a while now, and the daily ten-minute treatments were beginning to wear on him. He hated having to be driven back and forth to the hospital every day. He hated the way the radiation made him feel—tired and nauseated and "stupid." He hated losing his hair. He hated being taken out of school and given private tutoring at home. Mike tried to call whenever he could, even if it was just for a minute, to offer some kind of distraction for Tim and some kind of comfort to Sally.

Mike hoped like hell that the applause at the end of the town hall meeting meant that Altus was really ready to go. Because, ready or not, the starter pistol had gone off, and his favorite runner needed some real help from the team.

Chapter 8

REACHING PHASE II

*I*f Mike's life were a movie, the next four months would have passed as a montage of plane flights, ticking clocks, and calendar pages being torn off and dropped to the floor. His life was a blur of travel between Pennsylvania and California, meetings on Supragrel, updates with Tim's doctors, tearful and hopeful and painful talks with Sally, more meetings about Supragrel, emails and videochats with Tim whenever he could grab a minute to close his office door, more meetings, and on and on. Mike and Sally spent every spare minute they had researching Tim's condition. They found more and more research that suggested that the treatment Tim was receiving, while the best *conventional* treatment available, might not be the best *treatment* available. Sally began to work with a support group of other brain tumor sufferers and survivors to research supplements for Tim and to explore alternative treatments. If he was under a death sentence, what real risk was there in trying mushroom extracts that had worked in Japan, or antioxidants that had worked in small studies?

Most of the time, Mike was so tired and busy and worried that he wasn't quite sure where he was until he got into his car in the morning. The black Audi meant he was at home with Tim and Sally, and he should drive to the hospital, the doctor's office, or a support group meeting. The silver Mercedes meant he was in Chesterton and he should drive to the office. Today was a silver Mercedes day.

The Supragrel team had decided to meet every week to discuss status. Each team member gave Mike their updates by Friday at the end of the business day. He then used the weekend—usually the time spent on flights to and from California—to analyze the project schedule. By consistently reviewing the Critical Chain, he'd found that, in this project as in every other project he'd worked on, some tasks that weren't formally on the Critical Chain were very close to it. Identifying those and keeping an eye on them was essential.

Every Monday morning the team met for updates at 7:30 A.M. Those meetings, scheduled so that all the team members could hit the work week up-to-date and ready to run their lap of the relay, allowed the team to work through the most immediate deadlines and to clarify who was doing what. Most importantly, Mike always used the meeting to alert team members who were about to receive input from other members who were ready to finish and pass on their Critical Chain tasks. Managing these handoffs was crucial for speed. With fair warning, people were able to reschedule personal and office commitments so they could focus on their Critical Chain task when they got the baton.

For the Supragrel team, "passing the baton" wasn't a metaphor anymore. Trent, the lead physician on the team, was a former college track and field athlete at Villanova. One night over drinks, Mike learned that he'd trained under Jumbo Elliott, Villanova's star coach. Early on, Trent had brought in a real baton to one of the Monday morning meetings. Laughing, he'd tossed it to the person who was in the hot seat to deliver a task that week and told him he'd better run. It had become something of a tradition among team members now to literally pass the baton when they passed a Critical Chain task to the next person in line. No one was quite sure who had decided to display it prominently on his desk while working, but it had made the baton a signal for other team members and for Altus as a whole. People who had the baton on their desks received special treatment. They were exempt from going to meetings that were not essential to their Critical Chain task. They weren't expected to return emails or phone calls right away. While this had a few unintended consequences and ticked off a few managers who were used to making everyone jump when they walked by, it helped to clarify what Mike meant by Altus giving its people the ability to do focused work.

The kind of focused work, creative thinking, and good humor that spurred the use of a real baton was becoming a hallmark of Mike's team. That meant that, after three months, the fever chart for Supragrel looked good. The two time-savers the team had come up with in their early meeting—changes in manufacturing and in analyzing the Phase I samples—worked for the most part. Manufacturing got the drugs produced for the Clinical Trial using the open slot that they had found. There had been a slight delay in shipping the materials back to Altus, but it had resolved quickly, before the task even showed up on the Critical Chain. Clincal's strategy of analyzing the samples in smaller batches had worked, and that work was on the Critical Chain. The teams had lost one week of time because the head lab tech caught the flu. Processing was delayed for a week, and the writing of the final report couldn't resume until all batches were processed and analyzed. As a result, the team had experienced a bit of buffer consumption. All in all, the project was comfortably in the yellow on the fever chart after three months. They'd used up some buffer, but there was a lot left. And everything was going so much faster than anyone other than Mike had thought possible.

So Mike felt pretty good when he entered the meeting room at 7:15 A.M. and logged on, getting ready for the usual Monday morning update. Most of the Supragrel team members were already in the room, drinking their coffee and trying to wake up. "Good morning, guys." The tone had certainly become a bit more casual over the last months. "No surprises over the weekend. We are pretty much on track. If I look at the Critical Chain now we are getting ready for protocol writing. It looks like that will be done by the end of next week. The review committee has been scheduled to meet for review of that protocol two weeks from Thursday. Any comments?"

Karl, one of the writers, raised his coffee cup in a joking salute. "Yeah, Mike, we've already written a draft for the protocol. I think I can get the final written by end of this week—but only if it would make a difference. I'd need to prioritize this for the whole week, push some stuff around, but it's workable." Mike glanced quickly over the schedule, eager to see how the good news could help the project. It looked like they could easily recover a week's worth of buffer time, if not more.

"Excellent. But, in order for this to have any effect, I'm going to have to get them to reschedule the review meeting. You guys know it's not easy to get all the executives in the same place at the same time. But let's go ahead and make writing the protocol a high-priority task. I'll get after the review committee as soon as we're done here. If I can't move the meeting I'll let you know, and you can move it back down your priority list. For now, though, the baton is yours."

Mike tossed the baton to Karl, who caught it easily. For the rest of the meeting the team ran quickly through the remaining work. At 8 A.M. they were done and ready to go. Karl left with the baton raised high, joking about the meetings he'd be skipping and the phone calls from management he'd be ignoring.

Laughing, and pleased to see his team in such good spirits, Mike went straight to Charlene, who was catching up on emails.

She smiled at his good humor and said, "Howdy, Superman, I hear good things about Supragrel. Also, I've been getting your fever charts every week. Looks pretty good. What can I do for you?"

"Well, I just came from our update meeting and we have an opportunity to pick up some speed. I'm going to need your help, though."

"What's up?"

"We're going to finish writing the protocol this week and then we'll be ready to submit it for approval. I need you to move the review meeting to next week. If the committee can review the document over the weekend, we can meet on Monday for final approval."

She looked up with a frown. "Next week, two-thirds of the committee is in a management retreat off-site in Hilton Head. There's no way we can find the time to do this. Anyway, I'd have to ask Stephen, my boss. He runs all of Altus Labs' research and development organization. This is his show. Monday is out of question, though. Most of us will just be arriving that day."

"We could be there Tuesday morning. I'd bring the physician and the team leader from Medical."

"I'm sorry, Mike. In the current climate we can't approve extra travel. You know all travel is getting extra scrutiny corporation-wide. Plus, I can't have you just showing up at the executive-level management retreat."

Mike thought about pointing out the irony of having an executive retreat in Hilton Head when all non-revenue-generating travel was supposed to be cut, but he didn't want to get sidetracked into arguments about general corporate idiocy. He wanted to solve his problem. Now.

"Okay. How about we arrange for a web conference? Those are very inexpensive. And no one has to go to Hilton Head who isn't there already. If you can get the committee to look at the protocol over the weekend, we could finish this thing next Tuesday morning."

"I can't promise anything, Mike, but I will touch base with Stephen. If I can talk him into it, I'll get it set up for you. I'll call you when I know where we are."

Somehow Charlene got the okay from Stephen to carve out two hours for the committee to get together Tuesday morning. That meant that Karl was definitely on the Critical Chain. He spent the week writing the protocol and by Friday afternoon he was putting the final touches on the document. Mike stopped by and helped a little by lending a fresh set of eyes to the proofreading.

By 3:00, the document was ready to be sent to the review committee with a firm request to read it over the weekend. Mike also planned to send out a meeting reminder in the form of eight relay-race batons he'd picked up at the sporting goods store. He was fairly certain they'd get his point across when the batons arrived in Hilton Head. He'd also packed up and shipped Karl's baton to Charlene. It was her turn to run a lap.

〰

Mike flew home that night, feeling satisfied that the protocol was ready for the review committee, and that he and Karl would easily be able to address any issues or complaints. This time, instead of using the flight to prep for the coming work week, Mike used the time to think about Tim. He was managing the radiation well, the doctors said, but it hurt to see his energetic son looking so tired and pale, and the night that Tim had emailed him and said that he'd been feeling too gross to eat any ice cream, Mike had been up half the night, wishing he were there.

He arrived home to find Tim happily settled on the couch, reading. Sally was stuffing envelopes at the kitchen table for a fundraising drive she was running for the Kids with Cancer support group.

"Working too hard, hon?"

"Probably. But you know how I am, Mike. I'd rather keep busy than just sit still and worry. And we're getting great responses to the drive. You know how much it's helped me to be able to talk to other parents about what's going on."

"I do. When I finally told people at work, it was like, I don't know, like losing 50 pounds overnight. I just felt like I could move more easily. And people have been great. They don't bug me for details every minute, but I can feel everyone pulling for us. And I can see how hard they're all working."

"I know. You get a diagnosis like this and you just feel so alone. Like your kid is the only kid who's ever had anything like this. Like you're the only parent who's gone through it. It's horrible knowing that there are so many other people suffering too. But . . . it's not as lonely, somehow."

Mike kissed Tim on the top of the head, kissed Sally on the side of the neck, and sat down to help stuff envelopes.

The next morning Mike finally got a chance to visit the Kids with Cancer support group that Sally had been working with and to meet the friends Tim had made there. There was Kylie, a two-year-old who had her thumb in her mouth and her blanket dangling behind her, and had stage IV liver cancer. Her mom quietly told Mike that they'd just been told that Kylie wouldn't make it to her third birthday. Twelve-year-old Anna was luckier. Her stage III Hodgkin's disease meant she had about an eighty percent chance at a cure. Will was a determined fourteen-year-old with bone cancer who was learning to adjust to a prosthesis after an operation to remove his lower leg. He told Mike that his chemo had "gone great" and that his doctor said he should be able to get back to pitching a baseball any time now.

There were so many more, just in that one little room, stuffing envelopes and making signs. Kids with brain tumors, with leukemia, with lymphoma. And they were all so young and so small and so filled with hope. Mike's head reeled. His eyes filled, and he had to step out of the room for a few minutes to pull himself together. Sally followed, checking to make sure that Tim was deep in conversation with Will about baseball and videogames.

"God, Sally, how do you stand it?"

She silently wrapped her arms around him.

"I mean it. How do you stand it? I thought I had the hard part here, since I have to be away from you guys while all this is going on. That's nothing. This is . . . how do you take it? Kylie . . . she's only two, for God's sake, and there's not a damn thing anyone can do to save her. She's going to be gone. And it's not fair."

"I know. We cry here a lot. But we laugh, too. Because the kids are smart and beautiful and funny, and we have to love them while they're here. No matter how long or short a time that is."

Mike leaned his forehead against hers, eyes closed in pain. "I just wish I had Supragrels for all of them. You know?"

Sally took his hand and they walked back into the room. Will's dad brought him a cup of coffee. If anyone noticed that Mike's eyes were red, no one said a word.

The weekend at home was over much too quickly. Mike went back to Altus deep in thought.

〰〰

The Monday morning meeting was quiet that week. Everyone was waiting for Tuesday and the review committee. No one was quite convinced the execs would have read the protocol, or that, if they had, they'd be ready to move it to approval in the course of the two-hour meeting they had scheduled. It felt like the team was holding its breath. When the webcams linked up on Tuesday morning, Mike laughed out loud to see Charlene sitting there, grinning, with her baton prominently displayed. The other execs had their batons out and visible as well.

"We got your package, Mike. And we got your message. We are not going to hold up your relay any longer than we absolutely must. Let's get to it."

In short order, Trent explained the protocol, while the committee posed questions and made comments. The team pulled up the document and made the changes as soon as they were suggested, so that everyone could see the edits happening and everyone would know that their concerns had been addressed.

At the end of the two hours, they were agreed. The protocol would be sent out one more time with a request for review and final approval to be sent by email. By Wednesday morning it would be done. The team looked at Mike as if he'd accomplished some kind of miracle. No one, they said, had ever gotten the execs to move that fast. No one, he pointed out, had ever asked them to.

Wednesday morning also brought Mike an email from Charlene that contained nothing but a tracking number from FedEx. He waited in the office until the final delivery of the day, just to see what she was sending. When the baton rolled out onto his desk he was pleased, but not at all surprised. And he knew he'd be passing it on first thing tomorrow morning.

They'd saved one more week on Supragrel. The project was back in the green. And Thanksgiving was just around the corner. Thanksgiving was usually Mike's favorite holiday. But this year, its arrival didn't mean pie and turkey and a day spent with friends and family. This year it meant that Mike and Sally had to make one of the most difficult decisions they'd had to face about Tim's treatment.

With radiation therapy complete, the next standard step was for Tim to have another surgical procedure called brachytherapy, during which radioactive seeds were placed inside the cavity created in Tim's brain by the surgery that had removed his tumor. This allowed a large and targeted dose of radiation to impact the tumor. The problem with the brachytherapy was that it usually caused collateral brain damage. Mike didn't like this option at all. The alternative was to use a combination of Supragrel and PCV—a standard chemotherapy drug for the treatment of Hodgkin's lymphoma and brain cancers like Tim's—to treat the tumor pharmaceutically. The problem with that was that Supragrel wasn't ready yet.

Mike and Sally spent night after night talking on the phone while working on their respective computer screens, researching brachytherapies and their side effects, and studying the timeline and fever charts for Supragrel. Brachytherapy would offer Tim a few more months of life, probably, but equally probably those months would be months where he would be too disabled to do any of the things he loved. Supragrel, if it worked, if it was ready in time, offered so much more. More than once Mike sifted through Supragrel's Critical Chain tasks. According to the last update, the team was on track to deliver by Christmas, maybe even a little earlier.

Eventually, Mike and Sally left the consent form to start brachytherapy unsigned. They had faith in the potential of Supragrel, faith in Mike's ability and Critical Chain, faith in the team's ability to deliver on time. They would wait for Supragrel.

Chapter 9

THE BOARD MEETING

*E*arly in the second week of December, Mike called the Supragrel team in for a meeting. He greeted them all with a solemn nod, and silently turned on the projector he'd hooked to his laptop. A split screen appeared, with Tim and Sally seated on one half and Dr. Hart on the other. He turned and glared at the team.

"These are some of the people who've been depending on you. This is my wife Sally, my son Tim, and Tim's doctor, Dr. Hart. And they've been counting on you all of this time to push Supragrel out faster, to work harder, to run a better race, so that Tim and kids like him can get this drug sooner and start getting better."

He shook his head solemnly. "They've got one thing to say to you today."

He turned to the screen, and gave a whoop of triumph as Tim, Sally, and Dr. Hart hollered "Thank you!" with every bit of their strength. The team burst out laughing with relief and pride, and got to their feet to applaud.

Mike blew his family a kiss and turned back to his team. "You did it, guys. We're in Phase II. We're rolling out the clinical trial of Supragrel, and let me tell you, I think Charlene's still feeling a little faint from shock. You've done some incredible work and we're all grateful to you. You've set a standard that other people are really going to want to meet."

As the celebrating Supragrel team made their way out of the meeting room, Mike sat down slowly. They'd done it. They'd won the relay—this part of it at least. Timmy was one of the first patients receiving trial doses, and Sally was keeping Mike on almost hourly updates about how he was doing. They were both worried about potential side effects, worried that it might not help, and hoping like hell that it would. Though his relief over the project was enormous, Mike still felt like he was moving through the world holding his breath. While the team had finished their work with Supragrel, Tim's was only beginning. Every time Mike's phone chimed with a text message from Sally his gut clenched. And there was nothing for him to do but fight to focus on the work that needed doing.

Altus Labs couldn't stop talking about the speed with which the project had moved and about the guy who had gotten it to move that fast. It wasn't just a hot topic on the lab floors, either. Mike knew, when he got the invitation to attend a meeting in the rarefied air of the twelfth floor, that even the top brass were talking about Supragrel.

When Mike stepped through the two glass doors that led to the executive suites, he couldn't believe the hush. With no cubicles, there was no idle chatter filling the air. Instead there was the glorious and very expensive silence that could only be provided by thick carpeting, real wood paneling on the walls, and large offices with closed doors. On his way to Boardroom One, Mike paused by a few of the paintings, noting that unlike the humorous motivational posters that decorated his floor, the executives got real art.

Mike still wasn't quite sure what he was doing up here. The invite had come from someone he didn't know who had the unspecific title of "Executive Assistant," and there hadn't been enough time to catch up with Charlene or someone else who could fill him in on the details before he was scheduled to show up. It was uncomfortable walking in blind. It was all the more uncomfortable since Boardroom One turned out to be built to impress:

big table, big leather chairs, and big windows with an incredible view.

Charlene and Stephen, the VP of R&D, were already sitting in two of the chairs. Apparently they didn't think it would be a good idea to be late for this meeting either.

"Charlene, I didn't get much of an agenda for this meeting. What is this about?"

Charlene glanced at Stephen. "This is going to be interesting. Graham Fletcher, our CEO, heard about what's been happening with Supragrel in a briefing that Stephen gave him a few days ago. After the briefing, he ordered up a copy of the team report, reviewed it, and he wants to know all about Critical Chain."

Though it seemed a bit unusual for the CEO of a multi-billion-dollar company to pay so much attention to a single project, Mike was at least glad to be on familiar ground. As everyone down on his floor had already found out, he could talk about Critical Chain all day and every day, given the chance. And now that Mike knew it was Graham he'd be meeting with, he could put to use everything he'd heard about Graham and everything he'd noticed when he had seen a few of his announcements on Altus Labs' company TV.

Graham was taller in person, and quite thin. He carried himself with confidence. Mike shook hands and waited for the conversation to begin.

Graham leaned forward, intent. "So Mike, I've heard about Supragrel. Stephen gave me a strong briefing and told me a lot of good things about the project and about you. I gather we were able to move up this project by more than six months. How'd you do that?"

"The team did it. All I did was help to give them a fresh perspective on how they organize work. There were plenty of opportunities to make things faster. We just had to find them and understand what parts of the process were key to the actual delivery. We developed a better, more aggressive plan. The rest of the success was just the result of our relentless focus on execution."

Mike ran Graham briefly through the network build, giving the details of how manufacturing found some open timeslots that let them finish work earlier than expected. Unsure of how specific Stephen's briefing had been, Mike told him about the review meeting that had been conducted as a web meeting in order to save five business days. He noticed Stephen taking rapid notes while he spoke.

"I've seen the team report and the fever chart too, Mike. I've never had this kind of transparency for any project before. It's intriguing to be able to get such a close look at where everything is and how it's moving along, without having to be standing over my people's shoulders every moment. I think it's going to be really useful for us.

"I know you didn't come from the pharmaceutical industry, so now that you've given me a briefing, I want to give you one."

A briefing on the state of an industry from one of its leaders wasn't the kind of chance that came along every day. Mike was resolved to let someone else do most of the talking for a change, and learn everything he could from Graham. He was pretty sure he'd be needing the information.

Graham said, "This whole industry has a really nasty cold. It's called patent expiration. We file a patent for a molecule early, long before we know if there is way to make a drug based on it. Then we have twenty years' time to find out if that molecule can be used as a drug. It currently takes us twelve years to develop a drug and obtain the final regulatory approvals to sell it in the marketplace. This would leave us with eight years of patent protection, assuming we start the clinical research as soon as we have a molecule patented, which is most often not the case. Very often we have only a few years, sometimes even less, before we lose that protection. When we lose the exclusive rights to sell a drug, our revenues from that drug drop to zero almost overnight. There's an aggressive generics industry out there that literally ships out their versions of our drugs the day we lose protection.

From a patient perspective, it's hard to complain about that too much, since it gets medicine to people cheaper.

But it is a problem for us. Here is why. Our industry is highly regulated, and that means it takes us longer and longer to develop drugs, because the regulatory agencies' response times have gone up significantly. For us that means we have less time to market the drug exclusively. As I mentioned for most of our drugs, we only have a few years of market exclusivity to begin with. In those few years we need to recover not only our investment in that particular drug, but also make enough money to fund all the other projects that haven't made it to the final FDA approval. Essentially, the entire industry spends more money to develop drugs and has less time to generate revenue to gain back the initial investment. That means we have less and less money and time to invest in the R&D phase of new projects. This whole issue is becoming increasingly urgent. To put some numbers on that, the top twenty pharma companies worldwide are going to lose about one hundred billion in revenue over the next eight years."

Mike winced. "Yeah, that's a little more than a case of the sniffles."

Graham didn't laugh. "Altus is at the front end of this curve. We're anticipating losing twelve billion dollars in the next four years. The industry has a cold, but Altus Labs has pneumonia. In those four years the patents on several of our best-selling drugs will expire. We have to bring additional products into the market to replace them. Innovation made us one of the world's leading companies. Now we have to do it again. We have to accelerate our innovation process in order for us to keep our seat at the table. If we don't do that, we will have to consider dramatic steps. This could mean layoffs, selling portions of the business, or perhaps become an acquisition target."

Stephen raised his voice. "This is a dark scenario, but we think that Altus Labs can still have a bright future. Over the last four years we were very successful in putting together a new pipeline of drugs. Some of them have blockbuster potential. Others, like Supragrel, are niche market opportunities. They all can significantly help our patients. We're just running out of time to develop them. In particular, there's a group of late-stage projects that are critically important to us. When I talked to Graham about Supragrel, it's because we were wondering how to transfer its approach to project management to the rest of our portfolio."

Mike knew where Graham and Stephen were headed with this, but he let Graham make it official. "Mike, here's the question. What would it take to replicate Supragrel? Not just once, but through our entire portfolio? We have to accelerate our strategic Phase III assets while also moving the drug projects that are currently in Phase I and II ahead faster so that we can decide as soon as possible which ones are worth pursuing."

Mike had known that Big Pharma was going through some changes, but no one had outlined the picture quite this dramatically before. Graham stood, saying, "I want you to develop a plan for us. Stephen, Charlene, or anyone here in the room—including myself—will give you anything you need. I'd like you to think through the high-level strategy and come back to us in two weeks, if you can do it that quickly and still keep Supragrel on track."

Mike agreed. As the meeting broke up, he and Graham shook hands. As Graham left the room, Mike leaned over to Charlene and said, "You were right. This was definitely an interesting meeting."

Chapter 10

THE INTERVIEWS

*G*raham wasn't kidding when he said that Mike would receive any support he needed. Mike scheduled meetings with Stephen and all his direct reports. He'd never seen calendars cleared so quickly. Graham had apparently made it very clear to everyone that Mike's plan was top priority for everyone. No exceptions.

Mike was also given his first good look at Altus Labs' global R&D portfolio metrics. The numbers were not pretty. The metrics confirmed what Charlene had told him months ago: Only forty percent of their major milestones were met. The company had a decade-long track record of missing dates. Things had actually gotten increasingly bad over the years. Nevertheless, everyone at the company swore that missing a milestone date was a big deal. People lost their bonuses over it, after all. Regardless of the repercussions, Altus Labs' projects often ran late, that much was clear. The success of their flagship drugs must have cushioned them from their own inefficiencies for years.

Mike was looking forward to an in-depth interview with Stephen, who had been running Altus Labs R&D for the last three years. He'd started to work for the company immediately after finishing his M.D./Ph.D. Program. He was an excellent physician but thought that life as a doctor in the Boston suburbs, where he lived at the time, would be less exciting than a corporate research career. Over the years he had developed a great reputation as a researcher and had been involved in a number of successful drug launches. Of everyone at Altus Labs, he was the best-equipped to give Mike a real sense of what the pipeline really looked like and how severe Altus Labs' problems really were.

Sitting in the ever-popular Starbucks in Building One, now cheerfully decorated for the approach of Christmas, Stephen gave Mike a quick briefing on Altus's portfolio of drugs. "Our portfolio is significant compared to our direct competitors'. Altus Labs has about one hundred and fifteen drugs in Phase I and II. We also have about thirty-two molecules in Phase III. There are a number of Phase IV studies in progress for drugs that are already on the market. With those studies we're trying to find and confirm additional uses or 'indications' for particular drugs. Sometimes a medication that's prescribed for cholesterol, say, can have useful effects on stress or on heart problems. Overall, we have about fifteen thousand people working in R&D. About a third of Altus's workforce is in my department."

One hundred and fifteen drugs in early development seemed almost unmanageably high to Mike. He knew that Altus was very proud of the breadth of its early-stage pipeline. But he also knew that people within the company had told him that they were assigned to so many of these early stage projects that they didn't know where to begin with the work.

"How did Altus Labs end up with such a sizeable early-stage portfolio?"

Stephen paused and took a sip of coffee before he answered the question. Mike could tell he was preparing to answer very carefully and very diplomatically. "The portfolio growth predates my time as R&D leader. Seven years ago, Graham, in conjunction with my predecessor, established a management metric that pushed for fifteen new molecules a year, every year, starting with Phase I. Since they began that metric, we've doubled our early-stage portfolio. In order to hit the numbers, we introduced lots of new molecules. Also, we revisited older molecules that we had already analyzed for other purposes."

Mike raised an eyebrow, picking up on most of what Stephen had carefully left unsaid.

"So, Stephen, are all these early-stage drugs here because they're valid prospects or are they just here to comply with a business metric?"

"Well, I wouldn't like to call any of them invalid. You can't forget the serendipitous nature of R&D. Pfizer's Viagra is a great example. It started out as a drug that they thought would treat heart problems. After some early studies, they changed the indication. The rest is history. Any of our drugs could turn out to be something interesting." He paused again. "However, if you really put me against a wall, then I would give only a subset of our early-stage pipeline true priority."

"So, why this massive push? Why did you guys introduce so many R&D projects into your early-stage pipeline?"

"You heard Graham in the boardroom. We need to replace revenues that we know we're going to lose in the next few years. Laxaar, our flagship drug, is the number one product in the market for drugs to treat depression, and it will expire three years and nine months from now. We've all known for a long time that the clock was ticking."

Mike knew that this was as much as Stephen could say without risking his job. The bottom line was that Altus Labs had introduced a sizeable number of new projects in an attempt to have as many chances as possible to replace Laxaar by the time its patent expired. The company had to keep a lot of cash on its balance sheet to cover expensive clinical trials and other R&D work. The workload for people in R&D was increasing rapidly, and the old mentality of sticking slavishly to milestones hadn't changed. People in the R&D trenches were pushing back by negotiating timelines with plenty of padding built in.

Because the timelines were getting longer as a result of all the padding people were keeping to protect themselves, their milestones, and their bonuses, individual managers were pushing harder and harder to get their pet projects treated as high priority. But Mike had learned that anything could be called a priority. The push for new drugs meant that any Phase I or II drug could claim to be a priority. Because new revenue always had priority, Phase III drugs which were closer to market readiness were also priorities. The same went for any drug undergoing a Phase IV study, because a successful outcome meant the prolongation of an existing patent, which is the dream of every company in the pharmaceutical industry. And there were more "strategic" initiatives, for example a recent drive to improve the pipeline in oncology.

All this meant that over the last few years, Altus Labs had wildly increased the number of projects in the works without creating any real prioritization scheme. As a result, people in R&D were multitasking like crazy because they didn't want to be seen as uncooperative. No one at Altus Labs liked to say no. Instead, they added time to schedules and played that old familiar game of Schedule Chicken.

Meeting with Charlene a little later, Mike wanted to find out what she thought about Altus's project management. He trusted her to be as blunt as ever and give him her honest analysis as she'd always done before.

"Charlene, it looks bad. You know that. The metrics for R&D back up what you told me. We miss our milestones sixty percent of the time, and we've been doing it for ten years. Everyone says milestones are crucial, but we never make them. Can you tell me what's going on? What are the consequences of being late around here? Are there any?"

She nodded glumly. "I know those numbers. They're awful."

She continued.

"If we miss milestones, we develop a string of synchronization problems within the company. We miss manufacturing slots. We have agreements with external partners that need to be re-written. Sometimes we have to pay our partners for not working because we have agreements in place that commit us to a certain schedule of payments. Since a delay in a milestone means a delay getting a drug to the market, and since our patent expirations are set, milestone delays mean we have less time to make money from a particular drug. That negatively affects our ability to produce profits, which affects our stock price. We hate looking bad to Wall Street. And that's just the money side. I don't need to tell you that a delay in a major milestone means that our patients get their medicine later. That can impact the lives of millions and millions of people. It can impact the life of your son. So, yes. It's a big issue."

Mike probed further: "Obviously, project management is in the middle of all of this. How much of that issue is the result of problems that reside in the project management organization itself?"

"Well, we're in the middle of it, obviously. Eventually, we have to pull the projects together and make sure that everything is happening on time. It's a challenge."

"So, what's holding you up? Because I know you well enough to know this must drive you nuts."

Charlene glanced at Mike, then quickly looked away. "We don't own the resources. As you know, Altus Labs is a heavily matrixed organization. We depend on our counterparts in the different functions to be willing to cooperate. And we've only got limited visibility into what is going on there. Your Critical Chain reports on Supragrel are the best I have seen in terms of showing everyone's real status. But we don't have that on any of our other projects."

"Okay. But sometimes you do get things done. Sometimes you don't. Is this a project management maturity problem?"

Charlene paused. Mike seemed to have perfected his ability to make people at Altus pause and edit themselves before talking to him. "My team has some very talented and experienced project managers. I'd say about ten percent of the group are rock stars. Everybody wants to have them leading their projects. They get the job done. Then, I have about ten percent in my group that I'd rather not have. Eighty percent are somewhere between okay and good. They're solid but not exceptional. What I need is more rock stars. We keep buying new software, but I think we're chasing the wrong problem. We don't need new tech. We need better processes, and we need people who can execute them consistently."

Mike understood. This was the reason she was interested in Critical Chain and his experience at Versa in the first place.

He said, "The things that we have to do to turn this ship around are not going to be what people want to hear. I'm going to make a proposal that I believe in. If Graham doesn't like it, there's not much more that I can do here, and he'll probably fire me. Because, I have to tell you, I look at the mess you have here and I almost want to say it's impossible. And if I feel that way, Graham's going to . . . well, you know."

He didn't need to continue. Charlene nodded her understanding and they headed back to work.

Mike had a few other interviews with senior executives of Altus Labs. The last one was with Graham. They met in Graham's spacious office just down the hall from the boardroom. Graham seemed a bit more relaxed around Mike, now that he'd had a chance to see him hard at work. He asked about Mike's family and about his experience at Versa. They talked about life on the West Coast compared to the East. Mike wanted to know how Graham ended up running Altus.

"Believe it or not, I started out here. Working at Altus was my first real job. I came out of school with a double degree in organic chemistry and medicine. I began in the Labs as an intern working on prospectus molecules. That was over a quarter of a century ago. After I finished my Ph.D., I went straight to Altus Labs. The thing is that as a practitioner in the medical field you see perhaps a few hundred patients a year you might be able to help. It was always more intriguing to me to develop drugs and treatments that could help millions of people."

"Well, the company has certainly been very successful." Mike had studied the company history. There were some rave reviews of Altus Labs he found online. In the hallways, there were oversized pictures of the teams who launched successful drugs like Laaxar. Quite a few of the drugs he heard about most often had gotten their start at Altus Labs.

"Yes. We've done some really good work. The company has a history of stellar research. Some of the brightest scientists decided to come work for us. We pride ourselves on giving people a lot of autonomy. That was a big reason why we were able to attract a lot of talent early on. We encourage them to work on what interests them. You see the benefits of that yourself. Of course, you always need a bit of luck to make a strategy pan out. We were fortunate in that regard."

It was after 5 P.M. on a Thursday evening. Mike didn't have any plans. Apparently, Graham was not in a rush either. So, Mike kept the conversation going.

"So, things have changed over the last year. We were talking about Altus Labs having pneumonia. You mentioned the patent expiration issue. Can you elaborate on that?"

"Sure. In my estimation, the times of the easy discoveries of blockbuster drugs are over. The industry found treatments for major diseases. Today we have at least twenty major pharmaceuticals that address just a few of the same medical categories: cancer, diabetes, cardiovascular diseases, depression. We are more likely to find new drugs for more specific diseases that are not necessarily mass-market products. Even if we find a big drug again, we're likely to have other competitors in the market. We make less revenue per drug as a result.

"Also, the drugs are increasingly scrutinized by regulatory agencies here in the U.S. and elsewhere. This isn't a bad thing. But it leads to prolonged R&D development cycles. It takes longer for drugs to get approved. Combine that with the fixed patent time, and we have another reason why we get less revenue per drug.

"Now, if you look at our balance sheets and annual statements, it's not directly apparent why this all is really an issue. But it takes more than 1.5 billion dollars to develop a drug now, and I don't see that number getting smaller. Going into Phase III is a huge gamble for us as a business, yet we have at best a one-in-three success rate. There are no guarantees. We could have ten drugs in Phase III and all of them could fail. If something like that happened we'd have spent hundreds of millions, perhaps billions of dollars for nothing. Worse, we wouldn't have anything to replace the revenue that we know we'll lose because of expiring patents. We need revenues to continue our research. The drugs that make it to market don't just need to recoup the investment we make in that particular drug. They also need to recoup the investment in all the other drug projects that never will be a product."

Graham looked like just talking about this gave him a headache. Mike could see why.

"So this has to be a real threat to Altus Labs."

"Yes, and we can't simply raise prices as we wish. There is a lot of consumer concern about the costs of health care. There's a growing feeling of resentment about big pharma as part of that, too. The last thing we can do is to simply charge more. So, it's hard to see how we can continue to fund our current business model."

"So, how do you get around all this?"

"Well, that's the question for us: How much research should we finance internally? At the end of the day, there will always be more researchers than we can possibly hire. So, we have to think about that. Today, scientists don't necessarily assume they want to work for big pharma. They start companies and obtain funding through private equity investors or the stock market. We have to learn how to use their work to help ours. We have to become more creative in the ways we find potential treatments. We need to look at alliances with these smaller more innovative companies. We could license promising molecules from those companies. Or we could simply buy companies. Our M&A team is constantly screening the market for potential acquisitions. Next year, we plan to make one or two of those transactions. Maybe we need to merge with another pharma company. Personally, I'm not a big fan of mergers, because they have the potential to distract both organizations for years. All these options are on the table. But at the end of the day, regardless how we acquire new research, from the minute we decide to work on something we need to be as efficient as possible. To tell you the truth, in the last years we have been very busy developing the pipeline. We haven't made any real progress in the quality and efficiency of our operation. We might even have gotten worse. It feels like we—and I include myself in that—tried very hard to fix specific issues. But we might have missed the forest for the trees. It's time to get some fresh perspectives."

"Well, I hope I can offer you that."

"I hope so, too. So, tell me how far you are with your analysis. When will I be able to hear your suggestions?"

"I'm ready. We can have our briefing next week. I don't think that some of these issues are all that difficult. Other industries had to deal with similar challenges and were able to succeed. But not everybody's going to be happy to hear what I have to say."

"Don't worry about that. We are not here to play pat-a-cake. The senior leadership team knows what is at stake. Don't expect to meet pushovers that fall quickly in line, either. I would like to ask you to be clear and precise. Allow my team to test you. Supragrel showed us something that I thought was not possible. I saw a lean and nimble project execution. If your plan shows us how we can do this on all of our projects, then that is what will happen."

Mike nodded.

"You know, Mike, I didn't come to work for this company twenty-five years ago to be the guy who hands over the keys to a competitor or to a private equity company that's simply planning to gut our operation. A lot of people work here. I feel responsible for them and their families. We have a lot of patients like your son whom we need to serve. I feel equally responsible to them. Time is of the essence for Altus Labs. We will make arrangements to discuss your approach next Monday. Thanks for helping us."

〰〰

"Hey buddy, I don't have too long before I have to go into a meeting, but I wanted to see how you're doing."

"Not too bad. I'm really glad to be off the radiation, and the drugs they've got me on aren't horrible. Oh, and Dad? You remember how I've been playing chess as part of my therapy?"

"Yeah. Gotta keep that brain of yours awake and busy."

"I know, but guess what? Yesterday I beat Mom and I beat my therapist!"

"Nice going! I'll get online tonight and we can play a few games. See if you can beat your old man yet. Sound good?

"It sounds great, Dad. Hey, when you get home for Christmas can I help pick out the tree again this year? You know Mom never wants to get one that's big enough."

"I know. Your Mom's a great lady, but she can't be trusted when it comes to Christmas trees. I think she'd actually get a fake one if we'd let her. But anyway, I wouldn't think of going without you. Ever."

Mike swallowed hard. It was so good to hear Tim sounding like himself again, even though there was still no way of telling if the new drug cocktail was working. But Mike knew that he'd told Tim the truth. Whether Supragrel worked for him or not, Mike would never pick out a Christmas tree if his son weren't there to help him.

Chapter 11

THE TURNAROUND STRATEGY

*T*he boardroom was full again. Charlene and Stephen were there. Graham was there. There were also some other faces that Mike hadn't seen before. His laptop was plugged into a top-notch projector. His cover slide was crystal clear and glowing on the large screen. Mike listened in on the light conversation about sports, the stock market, and German cars. He took a sip of orange juice. In five minutes he was going to light this place up. In sixty minutes he might not have a job here anymore.

Charlene rounded everyone up and got them seated. Then she reintroduced Mike and let him have the floor.

"Thanks, Charlene. The other day Graham used a metaphor that I found very interesting. He said that the entire industry has a cold but that Altus Labs has pneumonia. Well, I looked up the standard treatment for pneumonia: You take some pills, drink a lot of fluids, take something like Codeine for the pain, and you get a lot of rest. Nowadays, pneumonia is unpleasant, but we can get over it quickly. So please allow me to suggest a different, more appropriate, metaphor. Altus Labs is obese, perhaps morbidly obese. We are not talking about XXL obese. We are talking being overweight by two hundred pounds. Altus can barely walk. It is on a diet of fast food, soda, and chocolate chip cookies. This needs to change. We need to put Altus Labs on a health plan to get it back on track. Altus Labs needs to learn how to eat healthy. Altus Labs need to exercise. There won't be rest for anyone at Altus Labs. We are going to have to walk faster—even run—because otherwise we are not going to make it."

Mike paused. Some of his colleagues back at Versa had told him that, every once in a while, Mike opened a meeting like he was running over people with a truck. On the other hand, he realized this was the first meeting he'd been to at Altus where no one was texting, checking email, or surfing the web while the speaker talked.

"So, the first question is: Why are we so bad at meeting our commitments? We hit forty percent of our milestones. This company is full of Ph.D.s who've worked in this industry for a long time. You're smart people who know what you're doing. Yet, when it comes to key events like being ready to test a particular drug for the first time in humans when you say you'll be ready, you can't even keep your commitments half the time. If we were an airline, nobody would fly with us."

Mike knew that no one in the room was happy to be hearing this. Altus Labs was still seen as a successful business by many. The company was well-known in the industry. People working for Altus Labs were respected in their communities. In many ways Altus Labs was a success story. The problem was that what had brought the company to its current level of success wasn't going to do a thing to help it remain competitive in the future.

"You've been managing the whole company based on an elaborate milestone system. Everything has a milestone date. We have a date for the first tox dose and one for the first human dose. We have a date for deciding whether to market a product. We have a date when our drug will be on the market. Then, people break these milestones down further. There are mini-milestones that map out how we get, for example, from first tox dose to first human dose. This approach goes all the way down to the task level, where we have due dates for particular tasks.

"In my analysis I found that all these milestones have something in common. They are based on standard project templates that nobody really analyzes. When it comes down to it, the milestones and due dates you are using to manage your work are nothing but negotiated timelines. For management, nothing can be fast enough, so you try to get to aggressive commitments. For the people doing the work, it's important to hit commitment dates because that's how they make their annual bonuses. So they try to get the least aggressive commitments. Whatever dates we track in our milestone management system, they have little to do with reality. They certainly don't reflect timelines based on thorough analysis and they certainly aren't backed up by a project plan. They reflect a compromise between the miracles executives want and the wiggle room that the teams think they need, all facilitated by middle management."

Mike took a sip of water and looked around the room. There were no smiles, and it wasn't going to get better.

"The second major issue has to do with prioritization, or really with the lack of it. You have introduced a vast number of new projects into your R&D pipeline with the hope of finding the next few blockbuster drugs. At this point I don't know what the true capacity of this organization is. I can't tell you if you have too many projects lined up or not. What I can tell you is that for the people in the trenches here, there is no way to tell what is important and what is not. They are being asked to juggle lots of different project assignments. They are expected to do this, and they are expected to hit their due dates.

"Here is the problem. Humans are not good at multitasking. If I asked you to drive from here to Philadelphia at sixty-five miles per hour while having a meaningful phone conversation with one of the Wall Street analysts, you would probably do one of those things pretty poorly. If I asked you to do these things and also write an email to your staff about their annual goals and objectives, you would probably either give the wrong guidance to your organization, mishandle an important call with a key analyst, or crash your car. However, you routinely expect your scientists to juggle many projects. They have no chance to stay focused on critical tasks, because they really don't know what is critical."

Graham nodded silently. Mike's point was one of those things that was so obvious, it should go without saying. But when it didn't get said, it was easy to forget.

"The second undesirable consequence of all the multitasking goes back to my first point. People know that they will have too many things to do, so they push back on timelines. You ask them for a due date, they give you something as late as possible. Sometimes there's a little horse trading. Then you settle on a due date. Again, this date has nothing to do with how much work really needs to be done. I found that certain timelines for a document were measured in weeks, while the true touch time for creating and finishing the document was measured in days. You've created a perfect system to make everything take as long as possible, while not giving you any kind of real handle on how to manage your critical timelines better. All that extra time? All that padding? That's weighing you down and making you slow.

"Altus Labs' obesity is causing it to suffer. This is what we have to deal with."

Mike could see heads turning as he paused. Everyone in the room was looking at Graham. Several people were already closing their folders and capping their pens. Clearly they were expecting Graham to storm out of the room. But Graham stayed where he was and Mike charged ahead.

"So, how do we get back to health? It's actually simple. We need to go back to sound planning. Instead of negotiating timelines, we need to plan out the work that has to be done to get from A to B. Templates are not good enough. We need a planning process that can capture the subtle differences between one drug and another. Those plans need to give us a realistic delivery date for a project, and they need to tell us what kind of variability we might expect executing the project. You have all reviewed the kinds of reports that Supragrel has generated. We need this kind of visibility on every single project here at Altus Labs."

One of the executives leaned forward to ask, "But if we don't have milestones, how can we hold people accountable for their timelines? How can we make sure that they do their job?"

This was one of the most common concerns people voiced when they heard about Critical Chain. The moment people heard that it was okay to be late, they panicked. He answered promptly. "Well, we do hold people accountable. We plan our work, and we make things visible. People are still responsible for doing their jobs. But here is the difference. We won't force people to commit to dates when we all know that the nature of our work is hugely variable. When we force people to commit to dates, we get conservative estimates up and down the organization. Instead, we ask our teams to come up with realistic but aggressive task estimates. We ask them to hit those, when possible, but to know that if they estimated incorrectly, we've got some buffer built in to take care of them. By doing that, we encourage people to finish early, and we can take advantage of that. Since the whole project team owns the buffer, they work together to conserve it. That way we have more accountability on the team level, in addition to the increased visibility on the management level.

"If things take a little longer than expected, that's fine. That's why we have the project buffer. But then we track the impact and try to recover any time we lost. You've seen that with Supragrel."

Mike paused for a moment and looked around again. Graham still seemed very thoughtful. Others seemed polite but not very responsive. He continued on.

"Our teams need to have the ability to prioritize the work on their project. If a task is on the Critical Chain, our teams need to have permission to do anything they can to get that task done. If that means someone needs to skip a non-essential meeting, then let it happen. If a team member is working on multiple projects, she must be allowed to focus on Critical Chain tasks over work that is not yet on the Critical Chain. If someone must choose between two critical tasks, they need to be able to tell which belongs to the higher priority project. Just doing that much is going to eliminate many of our problems. Disciplined prioritization, all by itself, will boost our efficiency."

Another executive raised a hand and said, "I doubt that we're going to be able to get all of our drugs perfectly prioritized. How can we possibly prioritize correctly given all that uncertainty in this industry?"

Mike was thankful for this question, because it raised an important point, even though he was pretty sure the questioner hadn't meant to be helpful. "You're right. There will never be a perfect prioritization scheme. But right now you have none. Each of the fifteen thousand employees in R&D can develop his or her own priorities, and I guarantee you they won't look the same. As a result, you have a huge amount of multitasking, because for the people in the trenches it seems that priorities are constantly shifted around. So getting to even a reasonable shared prioritization would give you tremendous improvement.

"What you need is the relay race mentality we've been encouraging in the Supragrel team. We were able to substantially beat the previous timelines, because we relentlessly worked tasks on the Critical Chain with high priority and focus. We constantly looked for ways to regain lost ground. This has to be the mindset on all of our projects. If it is, you'll win. It's that simple."

Given Supragrel's success, it was tough to argue.

"So here's what needs to be done. The only people in Altus Labs who can establish a sense of priorities are in this room. I need your commitment to a process that will establish priorities for all the projects here at Altus Labs. I think we can get that done in one week. I'm not going to go over how we're going to do it right now, but I will say that the outcome of that one week will be a clear sense of which projects are most important for us as a company. We will have the portfolio ranked and we will have a mechanism to communicate our priorities.

"We also need to stop managing projects by this milestone system. We need to replace negotiated timelines with end dates that are based on solid plans. Our project management organization has a lot of talent, but we don't have the right processes in place to make our people successful. We need to train our PMs so that they can do what I did on Supragrel with every project. I need the top ten PMs in the company to learn how to teach, learn how to run projects, and learn how to go through team planning. It will take three to six months to get this initial group ramped up. They'll be trained on the job, while we are putting Critical Chain plans in place for our key portfolio projects. I think we'll need about a year to convert the entire project portfolio. We will need the help of a company I worked with at Versa. We will need their know-how about Critical Chain Project Management and their software suite. It's a big commitment, but the return on investment will dwarf any expenses."

The CIO of Altus, Ram Gupta, raised an eyebrow and asked a question. "We already bought an expensive Enterprise Project Management software suite just two years ago. Why can't we work with that?"

Mike nodded his head. He had looked at the software system the CIO was talking about. It was a nice piece of software with a fancy user interface that Altus Labs used to manage its milestone data.

"I've looked at the package. It's a great example of standard Enterprise Project Management software. It does a lot of things. You can manage your milestones in it. It ties to the financial planning system. There are alerts you can receive on your cell phone. Here is what it doesn't do: It won't give you faster projects. We need a combination of software and process that lets us support the Critical Chain methodology and the 'relay race' for the whole company. There is really only one viable solution out there."

Ram was not ready to give up yet. Spending money to replace systems they already had was not appealing. "We've probably already invested about forty million in our current EPM solution. What makes you so sure yours is better?"

Mike decided to answer his question with a few of his own.

"Does your EPM system come with a process to take an organization from nothing to a full rollout of a consistent project management process? Does it have training and certification for project teams and project managers to create an organization that can consistently execute good project management? Does it allow you to communicate buffers and fever charts and identify the Critical

Chain of a project? Have any of their customers reported double-digit cycle-time improvements in their lines and a ninety-five percent or higher on-time delivery rate?"

Ram shook his head silently. Mike continued on.

"Believe me, I scanned the market. If I could do it in any other way I would. There is no better alternative. It's the best. And make no mistake, the Critical Chain software is only the catalyst. This is about changing your corporate culture. If we want to successfully turn into a culture of diligent planning and stellar project management, then we need a Senior Leadership Team that is engaged in the process. We need your critical thinking, your endorsement, and your ability to lead change."

Graham had lost a little of his distinguished appearance as the meeting progressed. He was well aware, as was everyone else in the room, that a lot of decisions he had made or authorized had led to the situation Mike outlined. He had also approved the budget for the EPM system two years ago. He thought it was a good idea at the time. Except it didn't move the needle for them. Graham raised his voice for the first time this morning.

"Mike. Thank you for your analysis. I think we all appreciate your candor. Can I talk to you for a minute?"

~~~

They walked out of the boardroom. To the left there was a door that led to the rooftop terrace. They had a wonderful view from there. It was a gorgeous day: a good day to be fired, if that was going to happen, but a much better day to be a success. Mike waited to see what kind of day it would be.

"Look, Mike. This has been very eye-opening for me. I like your obesity metaphor. I agree, we have become complacent. We are definitely too slow. So thank you for the straight talk. Look, I know you want to be back home with your son. I also know that you can help this company. I probably don't appreciate all the details of the plan that you outlined, but I believe in you. And I agree, we need to start the health regimen or we'll never keep the company together."

Mike just listened.

"We have dozens of drugs that can help millions of people like your son. We can make a difference. If we disappear, some of those drugs will, too. If we're sucked into a merger, a lot of people would lose their jobs. A lot of projects would be slashed."

Mike knew that Graham was right. Graham had talked about the possibility of a merger. Given Altus Labs' pipeline, they would be the first to get absorbed if the revenues couldn't be maintained by new drugs.

Graham continued. "Here in the Philadelphia area alone are at least three different companies that would like to gobble us up once our market value is down fifty percent or more. I don't want that to happen. I need you on my staff. I want you to implement this plan. Not some people we don't know brought in from the outside."

"Look, Graham. My son is . . . I don't know if he will see this through. This is going to be a tough decision for my family."

"I know. We will do everything possible for you to see your son as much as you can. I have a corporate jet that can take you to California on the weekends. We can relocate your family if you prefer. Whatever you need, I will make it work."

Mike nodded. "Obviously, I want to say yes. But I have to talk to my family. Let me fly home for Christmas. This isn't the kind of thing I can decide alone. I'll give you my answer after the holidays."

That night, while Mike got ready for his flight, he and Sally spent some time on the phone, talking over the job offer. A few minutes into the conversation, Mike paused.

"What's up, sweetheart?"

"I didn't want to tell you until you got home, Mike, but . . . Kylie died this morning. Her parents were with her the whole time and she didn't suffer and . . ." She broke down into silent weeping. Mike knew she was fighting not to scare Tim, who was already grieving for the loss of the tiny girl who'd always managed to find a smile for him.

"Oh, Sal . . ."

"I know. And I'd say, 'I can't imagine how they must feel' . . . but I imagine it every single day."

"I have to take this job, you know. I already knew I was going to. But I have to take it, Sally. I don't have a choice here. I always knew that Supragrel wasn't just about saving Tim. I always knew there were other sick kids. But now they have names. And faces. And they're dying. And I can't go back to working on semiconductors when I could be working for those kids."

"Of course you can't. And nobody should ask you to. Tim and I certainly won't. We'll get him through his treatment and we'll come out there to you. You knew we would."

Going to Kylie's funeral was one of the hardest things Mike had ever done. He and Tim and Sally held tight to one another's hands, crying helplessly. Afterward, it was a grim and silent ride home. The Christmas decorations all over the house seemed an insult to the loss they all felt, and the devastation they knew Kylie's family faced.

They sat in the living room, staring blankly at the tree. No one knew what to say.

It was Tim, the one with the most reason to be scared and sad, who eased their pain.

"So, Dad?"

Mike looked up, wiping his eyes furtively.

"I hear you get to borrow the private plane, right?" Tim was looking at Mike sideways, trying to charm him into a smile. "Do you think that maybe, you know, if you get really busy and can't fly out here one weekend, maybe Mom and I could fly out to see you? Because it would be . . . efficient! And, you know, you're all about efficiency."

Mike laughed, as much from the joke as from the release of tension. Clearly, even if Tim's brain was still healing, it was working just fine. "That's a fairly persuasive argument. I'm pretty sure I can talk Graham into at least letting you go for a ride sometime."

"No way!? Really?"

"Really."

Mike hugged Tim hard. They both kissed Sally, and then talked for another hour about the plane and Tim's plans for it, about the upcoming chess tournament with some of the kids from his support group, and—more seriously—about the MRI that Tim had coming up soon.

Later that night Mike sent a quick email to Graham. He accepted the position with the condition that he be allowed to take a full week at home for Christmas. Eight minutes later, Graham replied with a quick message from his phone. It said, "Great!"

They had an agreement.

The next morning Mike received a call. It was Stephen. They exchanged the usual holiday greetings, then Stephen got right to the topic.

"Mike, Graham told me that you agreed to lead the rollout. I'd given you a strong endorsement so I'm really pleased. I know you want to take some time off and I know it's the holidays, but there is one thing I need to talk with you about."

Mike was interested to find out what Stephen was driving at. "Go ahead. I've got a bit of time to talk."

"Let me be frank with you, Mike. It is not a surprise to me that you and Charlene get along so well. You both like to do what is right. When you feel like you've got the right answer to a problem, nothing holds you back. When Charlene hired you, she hand-carried the job requisition form to our CFO to obtain his signature. That's how she got you in here so fast. We normally don't hire people within twenty-four hours."

Mike chuckled a bit. He remembered how fast this process had appeared to him that time.

"You've clearly got Graham's and everybody else's attention. With you on board, we have an opportunity to make a potentially game-changing impact here at Altus. But I don't want this to come across as a power play led by Project Management. I have a lot of talented people working for me. Scientists. Experts in their fields. They all have contributed in their own ways in the past. They are valuable for the future of this company. For Critical Chain to succeed, we need their buy-in and their willingness to carry the methodology forward."

"Agreed." Mike was familiar with this problem. He knew that he could easily come across like a cowboy riding into town to solve everyone's problems . . . and that he could tick off a lot of good people in the process.

"So, how are we going to get buy-in?"

"Well, Stephen. Since this rollout will be centered around R&D, we need to put a steering team in place that probably consists mostly of your direct reports. We will use the steering team as a sounding board for the rollout."

"It's a good plan. I think you're right, too. I'd like to have all my direct reports on that team. You might have talked to some during your interviews. There is Craig Mollestun, the head of Altus's toxicology organization. He is a great guy. Easy to work with. You will like him. Then there is Kim Young. She is the head of regulatory affairs. Kim is new in my team. She came from a competitor two years ago. She has a fantastic network with the regulatory agencies. Then, I'd like to include Gerd Schmelting. He is head of manufacturing. Gerd doesn't report directly to me. He and I report to Graham. Finally, there is Joseph McCullen, head of clinical operations. Joseph is a terrific guy. He and Charlene have had a few disagreements over the last few years. The Clinical Project Managers in Joseph's organization report dotted line to Charlene. She feels he could do more operationally. Joseph thinks there is too much on people's plates, and he doesn't like Charlene's intensity. I need Joseph to be on board for this to work. They might be a bit tricky, but I'm sure you can figure it out."

"And, of course, Graham and Charlene will be on the team as well," Mike added.

"Well, that goes without saying."

Mike nodded. "I think I'd better have one-on-one meetings to level-set with all the steering team members as soon as I return to Chesterton."

Stephen said, "Makes sense. Graham and I will send an email around that they should expect your call. I appreciate that you are doing this."

"No problem. It needs doing."

"That's right, Mike. Merry Christmas."

The suggested members were notified that day by an email from Graham and Stephen that the rollout of Critical Chain was on its way. They were asked to meet with Mike in the new year to get up to speed on the specifics of the new plan. Given the busy traveling schedule of everyone, it would take a few weeks for all of them to get together as a group. Mike requested Bob Gabriel as the new Project Manager for Supragrel. He trusted Bob like nobody else. Charlene made it work.

The Knights settled in for a quiet family holiday. With the loss of Kylie so painfully fresh, they weren't going to have the merriest Christmas on record, but like Sally said, they were going to remember to love each other now—no matter how much or how little time they might have to do it.

Chapter 12

FIRST THINGS FIRST

*P*eople at Altus Labs did a lot of talking about priorities. They'd brought in consultants to give an entire leadership course on prioritization. Managers were constantly reminding their teams about "having your priorities straight." The problem was that Altus Labs had no real priorities. Anything that the company did could be positioned as a priority.

Mike needed to start the new year fast and start it right. He didn't have much time to sift through the real priorities and the fake priorities, the priorities that mattered to management versus the ones that mattered to the teams or the patients or the marketplace. He needed a fast and reliable method for setting some priorities that would be taken seriously. So he asked Graham, Stephen, and Charlene to make time for a one-day off-site meeting. After a little thought, he decided to invite Ben Clark, head of the Portfolio Management Organization as well. Graham's assistant suggested using Graham's golf and country club, but instead Mike booked a simple conference room at a Marriott across town. Nobody was going to be distracted from this meeting by running into old friends in the restaurant or taking a short break to grab a little practice at the indoor driving range.

Mike got there early and prepared the room by putting up posters on all four walls showing all hundred and fifteen Phase I and Phase II projects, the thirty-two Phase III molecules, as well as the eighteen drugs the company currently had on the market. At 8 A.M. he greeted the leaders of Altus Labs.

"Happy New Year. Thanks for coming this morning. I know it's not easy to clear your calendar for a whole day, so I really appreciate your making this a priority. I appreciate it all the more because Altus Labs truly is not as good as we hope to be at managing our priorities. That's why you are here."

Mike paused briefly to let his words sink in and then continued. "As I've talked to people here at Altus, they've told me that they can justify anything they want to do, any pet project they have, by tying it to something that one of you has expressed an interest in. We've already talked a bit, in the boardroom, about why this is a problem. Today, we need to start fixing it."

Graham's eyes narrowed. Mike could practically hear him wondering why he'd hired Mike in the first place.

"What I'd like to do today is to go through the entire portfolio. I've got it up here on the wall for you. You'll rate each drug in three categories: science, strategy, and revenue potential. On science: Is this drug truly innovative, or is it a "copycat" offering that already exists somewhere else? On strategy: Does a drug support our commitment to oncology, diabetes and weight management, and neuroscience, or not? Last but not least, revenue. What is the revenue potential for a particular drug? We will use a very simple rating mechanism for this. Every drug will be rated in each category. We will use green for high, yellow for medium, red for low."

Mike had red, yellow, and green Post-it notes. He passed them around.

"The group has only one vote per category per drug. So, you need to come to some sort of consensus."

Graham cleared his throat. He looked uncomfortable and maybe a little shy in this unusually small group. This exercise was clearly not the executive retreat he was used to. "Look, Mike. We don't have the answer to every question. I don't know everything about each of these drugs and the science behind it. And each one has a significant chance of failing. How can I make a reliable decision without all the information?"

Mike had expected that concern to come up.

"Well, Ben and I did a little bit of prep work leading up to this meeting. The black binders in front of you have a quick summary of each drug. There is a page on the science of the drug, including a review of current drugs in the market, as well as an estimate of the possible revenue, incorporating estimated probabilities of success. Also, we have alerted all your direct reports that they'll be getting calls from you throughout the day looking for information. They'll take your calls anytime."

"Right, but that's about one hundred and fifty projects to go through," said Stephen. "Even if we only spend four minutes on each drug, we'll be here for something like ten hours." He sounded a little cranky.

"As far as I am concerned there's no limit to how long we stay here. The room service is decent. You can't possibly have anything more important to do than saving the company. And I'm perfectly ready to be here tomorrow as well, if that makes sense."

Mike smiled a little. This day was committed, and they had told him to get the job done. He would, even if they didn't like it.

"Okay. What do we call 'high priority' or 'green' on the scientific side? I want you to use that for any drug where there are no major developments at other companies and where there are no competing drugs already in the marketplace. Yellow is for a drug that other companies are working on, but that doesn't have competing drugs on the market. Red means there are one or more competitors in the marketplace already."

Graham interrupted. "Wait a minute, Mike. I think we are missing something here that's really important. It's great when we can create a drug that meets a need that's entirely unmet. But our biggest revenue potential isn't there. Our biggest revenue potential is in creating a new, more effective drug that beats out and replaces a drug that's already being used. The market's already there. Insurance companies and healthcare providers are already set up to cover the costs for their customers. We get paid a lot faster."

Mike paused, thinking that over. "That makes sense. It's the same thing in the tech field. You don't usually do as well inventing something people haven't ever had before. It takes too much time and money explaining why they should want it. You do a lot better making stuff that they already have—but making it better and more effective. Like the iPhone, right?"

Graham nodded, satisfied. "So, okay, let's say that we give a green to any drug that has the potential to be 'best in class.' That way we include the ones that break new ground in a certain treatment area as well as the ones that achieve superior results over existing drugs. Yellow is for a drug where we have a better-than-average chance to compete for the number two or three spot. Red for anything else."

Mike continued. "The next category should be very simple to determine: Does this drug belong to one of the major three areas we are focusing on? Is it in oncology, diabetes and weight management, or neuroscience? Then it's a clear green. If the drug represents an interesting secondary market it's yellow. If none of these conditions are met it's red. The last category is equally simple. Green means that, based on our current estimates, the drug has blockbuster potential—beyond one billion dollars a year. Yellow means the likely annual revenue is between two hundred fifty million and one billion. Red means the revenue potential is below two hundred fifty million."

The group got to work. They were startled to find that in less than two hours they were done with the Phase III projects as well as with Altus Labs' current products. It had taken much less than four minutes per drug for these, because they were well-understood entities. So far, two-thirds of the stickers they had used were green, but there were some interesting reds and yellows beginning to show up here and there. Mike avoided lengthy discussions, though. He encouraged them to make decisions quickly and instinctively. They needed to get this all out where they could see it.

"Good job. Now we only have to go through the hundred and fifteen Phase I and II projects. Should be a piece of cake." Mike thought maybe they'd decided not to kill him after all. Graham gave him a sideways glare, went to the buffet, picked a few grapes, topped off his coffee, and announced that he was ready for round two.

The dynamic quickly changed as the team approached this second set of drugs. It took much longer to discuss the projects. Graham and Stephen were starting to look into the binders, and they'd pulled out their cells to call the respective therapeutic heads of Altus Labs' R&D organization and subject matter experts a dozen times or more.

By five, they were about three-quarters of the way through the pipeline. Graham wanted to take a break. "Let's get some fresh air." They went outside for a quick walk through the park next to the hotel. When they came back, the hotel had brought out a light dinner and Charlene and Stephen were eating and looking exhausted. Mike offered an out for the day: "Do you want to finish up tonight, or spend some time on this in the morning?"

Graham clearly wasn't crazy about either option. He gestured at the wall, now loaded with Post-its, and asked, "What are you going to do with all this, anyway?"

"I have a transcription team coming in as soon as we are done here. They'll put the matrix up on an Intranet site overnight. If we finish up tonight, we'll have the electronic matrix up tomorrow by 8 A.M. I want you to take another look at this when it's more formally laid out. By noon tomorrow we'll open the site up to your direct reports and the CFO for their feedback. They have until the end of the week to talk to us about any changes they want. Based on the final version, we can develop a rank ordering of the portfolio by Monday of next week."

Graham nodded, ran his hands through his hair, and suggested that they keep going.

When they finished at 10 P.M. that night, there was a lot of red on the Phase I and II projects. They all knew what that meant, but it was a relief to have it out where they could see it. As they left the hotel, the transcription folks were already waiting in the lobby. Leaving the room last, Mike took an extra minute to find the rating for Supragrel. It was flagged green, green, and yellow. That was all he needed to know.

〜〜〜

"Hey honey, how did it go?"

"I think it went pretty well. You know how resistant these guys can be to change, especially when it means facing the consequences of their own past decisions. But I think we made progress."

"I'm so glad. Hey, I've got good news for you, too. We got Tim's MRI results today, and there's a substantial improvement. They don't see any growth in the tumor at all!"

"That's fantastic! Really? They're sure?"

"They're sure. They had a whole group of doctors look at the scans to make sure. They could hardly believe it, but it's working just the way they'd hoped. They're even starting to wonder whether they might start to see the residual tumor shrink over time. "

"I want to, I don't know . . . cry or sing or something. I can't wait to tell the team about this!"

"I know. Hey, we'll see you this weekend, love. Get some sleep, okay? Love you."

〰〰

The next morning, Mike picked up his cappuccino at 7:45 A.M. He sent a fast email to the team to tell them how well Tim was doing on their drug and was pelted with enthusiastic, relieved, and supportive emails from everyone almost as fast as they could type them.

Fifteen minutes later he was back to work, looking at the Altus Labs portfolio on the website. The list of drugs was finally sorted into some kind of sensible order. First on the list were the current products, then the Phase III drugs, then the Phase I and II drugs. There was a lot of red as he scrolled down. In places it looked like someone had spilled a can of red paint on the website. There was no question about it anymore. If you looked behind the curtain, the pipeline wasn't pretty. It was one thing to know this in theory. It was another thing entirely to have it in glorious Technicolor, out where everyone could see it.

Graham, Stephen, Charlene, and Ben had no further comments. What could they say? By noon Mike opened up the site to the Steering Team and the next level of management below them for review. He explained the color scheme in the email and made the information from the black binders available electronically. Half an hour after he had hit send, his in-box was flooded with replies—constructive, confused, panicked, the whole range.

Of the hundred sixty-five drug assessments, thirty-two assessments were challenged during the Friday morning review session Mike scheduled. The jury, made up *American Idol*-style of Graham, Stephen, and Charlene, found that they needed to make only nine changes to the color codes they had previously set. By Friday noon, they had their final prioritizations set and Mike was able to build a tiered list of the entire pipeline.

Of all the hundred sixty-five drug assessments, there were only twelve drugs that were all green, and four of these were already on the market. Better news was that in addition to those twelve drugs, the company was working on fourteen large products with blockbuster potential. But all of those had yellow in the science or strategy categories. Looking for a catchy name that would point out the potential speed and power of these drugs, Mike called them "Altus Labs' Eagles."

The substantial middle group was made up of the remaining drugs with at least mid-sized revenue potential, and with at least one green or two yellows in the science and strategy categories. Mike called them Blue Jays because they had the potential to make a big noise or to just be an annoyance. Altus had eighteen of these on the market, another eighteen in Phase III, and thirty-nine in Phase I/II). Supragrel was a Blue Jay.

There was a terrifying number of remaining projects that had low revenue potential or scored very poorly in science or strategy. Mike called those the Hummingbirds because, frankly, they were lightweights. Altus had allowed two of them to go to market. It was carrying six in Phase III and a depressing sixty-five in Phase I/II.

After ranking each of these groups of drugs within their categories, Mike was able to hand off the prioritization scheme to Graham and the Steering Team. By Monday morning they had it: a fully vetted prioritization scheme at Altus Labs. Graham followed up with a note to the Steering Team. In that note he reiterated the need to make Critical Chain a priority for the company. The acceleration of just the Eagles would be significant. Each of these projects had a potential value per day exceeding three million dollars. A ten percent cycle-time reduction on these twenty-six projects would be worth billions of dollars a year to Altus Labs. That was money that the company could use to finance its operation and fund future research.

Chapter 13

THE NEW GAME

*W*ith the prioritization scheme set, and with the state of the pipeline out there for everyone in management to see, it was time to get serious about fixing the things that had allowed the problems at Altus to get this far. Mike Knight had asked for Altus Labs' top ten high-potential people. If they had technical knowledge in the area of pharmaceutical research and development, process management expertise, or a project management background, those would be pluses, but they weren't the things that Mike was focused on. He wanted people with the ability to learn quickly, communicate effectively, and teach patiently. He wanted people who could deal with adversity, manage change, and lead others to do the same.

He didn't care where they came from in the company as long as they had those skills.

What he got was a superb group of people. Graham and the others had really dug deep into the organization to find him the people he needed. The group consisted of a number of Six Sigma Black Belts, a few director-level executives in their thirties who rightfully could expect to make it to VP in Altus Labs, and some very senior project managers from Charlene's organization. Bob Gabriel had called Mike's attention to a project manager from the Altus Labs' IT division. Even though IT was treated as something of a second-class citizen at Altus, Sandy Richardson's reputation was stellar. She had rescued a major SAP implementation within Altus Labs and was able to pull a project that was very late back on track. Mike would need people of that caliber. Bob promised to get Sandy up to speed on Altus's R&D processes in no time. Everyone in the group had been briefed on the Critical Chain methodology and knew what this initiative was about. It was up to Mike to fill them in on the tactical plans.

"We need to start by shaking our Eagles loose. We need to get them out of our pipeline and on to the market. In order to make this happen as quickly as possible, while you guys get on-the-job training in the Critical Chain method, we've retained some consultants to work with you on these, so nothing will fall between the cracks while you're learning. And you are going to be learning a lot in a short period of time.

"The consultants will show you how to lead a team through an effective network build. It's your job to learn how to help teams build tight networks. They'll also show you how to move a team into using Critical Chain behaviors. Once we're done with the twenty-six Eagles, the consultants are out of here. So use every minute of their time. You need to learn the process, and you need to learn the software. This is a huge opportunity, but it's not one you can afford to screw up."

Sandy Richardson, the project manager from IT, raised her hand and started to ask her question before Mike even said her name. "How much time do we have to tee up the Eagles in the Critical Chain methodology?"

Mike had liked her directness and her intelligence from the very first interview. "As little time as possible, of course." The group laughed, suspecting this wouldn't be the last time they heard that answer from him.

"I have budgeted four months, with two months of buffer, for these. By the end of that time I want you guys to be Critical Chain experts. That's the minimum time it takes to certify someone. But these are extraordinary measures because we've got extraordinary problems. You have been relieved from any other job obligations. For the next four to six months you will live and breathe this."

Mike thought they all looked excited and just a little anxious. That was probably appropriate. They all knew what this was about. They were all taking a giant gamble, and he was taking it with them. There was no other initiative like this in the company. If it worked out, they'd be stars. If it failed, everybody would know whom to blame.

Sandy continued, "That doesn't give us a lot of time to deal with buy-in issues. I can see that some team members aren't convinced that Critical Chain is the way to go. What's our plan for dealing with that?"

"Good question, Sandy. You're already seeing potential problems and thinking about how to solve them." Buy-in was always a problem with a new system, and Mike had encountered the same resistance among the teams at Versa early on.

"The consultants are going to be able to help you a lot with buy-in. They have the tools to prepare you for in-depth questions, and they have solid process expertise to lead teams through the planning and execution cycle. But you're right to be concerned. This is a change in the way we conduct business here. Some people will get right in line with this, some will take more time, others might even resist. So, all the Eagle teams will have an executive sponsor. That means you can expect that Graham, Stephen, or one of their direct reports will show up for kickoff sessions. They will personally explain to the team why this approach is so critical to the company. That ought to help, but if we can't overcome buy-in issues quickly, please let me know about them right away."

All this focus and all this management support had gotten his soon-to-be experts fired up. These people were hungry for an opportunity to show what they could really do.

"It's 8:45 A.M. now. We have arranged one-on-one meetings with your dedicated consultant at 9 A.M. Here are the pairings. Go grab some coffee, then get back here and be ready to run."

He handed out the assignment sheets to each of the candidates. They found the name of their mentor, a brief bio, contact information, and the room number for their first meeting. The real work was about to begin.

ᨃᨃ

The candidate experts didn't disappoint. After three weeks, the first ten project teams were up and running. They had developed Critical Chain project plans for their assignments. Reviews of the new schedules and approval of the resulting timelines were accelerated through upper management so that the teams could get moving as quickly as possible. Mike made sure that the governance committees were subordinating their meeting times to the project teams.

For several planning sessions, Mike dealt with the recurring theme of panic over having a project buffer. What will happen if management sees the buffer? Won't they just start cutting that buffer? Won't they simply expect us to deliver at the unbuffered end time? Those questions were put somewhat to rest when Mike pointed out that the Steering Team had been briefed on the buffer and how it worked. They all knew what the buffer was there for. No one needed to worry.

Four weeks into the new system, when February hit, there was suddenly a lot more to worry about than management yanking a few days from someone's buffer. Sandy Richardson from IT, who had done an excellent job on her first network build, was working with her second team. It had the code name FOX7 and was a major breakthrough for delivering insulin. It was a cream rather than an injectable drug. In the past there had been numerous attempts to replace the delivery of insulin via needles with something that was less invasive. A few years back, two large pharmaceutical companies, Pfizer and Eli Lilly, had pulled projects off the market that were attempting to deliver insulin through an inhaler.

This new cream was a breakthrough. If it worked, it would be a revenue blockbuster for Altus. The network build had gone well. The team diligently accounted for the work that remained to be done. There was one last

Phase III study that needed to be completed. The team was just about to finalize the protocol for that study, which was scheduled to be carried out in fifty-five countries. Sandy's IT background made handling the software simple. But when she triggered the computation of the Critical Chain and the buffer, the team was shocked. It showed a buffered end date nine months later than expected.

"Graham won't like this!" said one of the team members. "We told him we would deliver this project by the third quarter of next year. Now we're talking the second quarter of the following year? He's going to kill us."

They reviewed the Critical Chain for the project over and over again, finding small changes to make here and there but no real time savings. Sandy called Mike during a break.

"Mike, I think we have something for you. And it's not pretty. Please come down."

Mike conferred with Sandy and her mentor about the network. Sandy had pulled out all the stops. One of the Critical Chain consultants had reviewed the schedule as well. The Critical Chain was credible. The team had modeled the enrollment process of all sites in all countries to get a detailed look at what was going on and what they could expect. The buffer reflected valid uncertainty and risk associated with the project. The task durations were even slightly more aggressive than those of other Critical Chain projects in development. This team was holding nothing back.

Mike nodded grimly. The team had done everything they could. Sandy had done everything she could. They were trying to clean up a mess they hadn't made, and it simply wasn't going to be possible this time.

"Okay. Let me take this further. I'll get back to you tomorrow. Good work on this guys, and thanks for getting it to me right away, Sandy."

Mike had known something like this would crop up. Whoever had made the commitment to deliver FOX7 by the third quarter of next year had based that commitment on faulty assumptions. Someone a few years back had just thought it sounded good and hadn't looked with any care or detail at the work that needed to be done. Most of Altus's timelines were bloated, but there were going to be some that were overly aggressive and FOX7 just happened to be one.

This was the inescapable result of "negotiated" timelines like Altus's. There was no real basis for any of the milestones. Once in a while a major project was recognized as super-important, and then milestones were moved because nobody wanted to stand in the way. And nobody had the means to tell what was possible and what was not. It was just another version of Schedule Chicken.

And they had been playing it with one of Altus's most important projects.

On his way to the elevator, Mike called Charlene to ask for an immediate and unscheduled briefing with Graham and Stephen on FOX7. Charlene said she would be happy to make a slot for Mike in their meeting that Thursday at 3 P.M.

Mike just smiled. "I need to speak to them this afternoon. Ideally, in the next thirty minutes."

Charlene laughed. Mike thought he heard a faint note of panic behind it. "They are in a financial review meeting to prepare for the next analyst call in two days. I doubt that any of them will step out. Those are crucial calls."

"It's about FOX7. What I have to tell them might change the flow of their next analyst call."

Charlene knew that Mike wasn't into dramatic appearances, much as she wished he were at that moment. This was real. "All right. Look, go to the conference room next to Boardroom One. I'll have both of them there. But Mike, this had better be justified. As much as Graham likes you and Critical Chain, he doesn't like wild stunts. Do not screw around with this guy."

Twenty-five minutes later Graham came into the conference room followed by Stephen. They were not smiling, but Mike didn't expect them to be. And he didn't expect them to be any happier when they left.

"Gentlemen, we have an issue that I need you be aware of. We've discovered that one of the Eagles is actually more like a wild goose, and we are on a wild goose chase."

Mike's introduction didn't do its usual job of getting people to laugh and relax. "What are you talking about?" Graham was clearly annoyed. He'd just been interrupted in the middle of a vital planning meeting, dragged over into the conference room with no explanation, and now Mike was trying to be funny? He crossed his arms over his chest, leaned against the wall, and glared.

"Previously we'd announced that FOX7 will be on the market by the end of the third quarter of next year. Now that we've taken the time to thoroughly analyze the work that needs to be done, we're looking at a delivery date that's about nine months later. With a little luck we can accelerate it. But it is extremely unlikely that this project will deliver by the end of next year."

Graham looked at Mike. "What does the schedule say exactly?"

"Well, the unbuffered end date is about the end of the third quarter of next year. We have gotten to that by creating the most aggressive schedule possible. The buffer is nine months. That's big, but it's not too big for a project that's this complex. Realistically, this is going to come in at the end of June the year after next. Maybe a little earlier if we're lucky."

"Why don't we take out some buffer? This is a pivotal project."

Mike thought, just for a moment, about ripping his hair out. He had explained that situations like this could occur. He had prepped the Steering Team, including Graham, for exactly this problem. Now, with the problem in front of them, it was like none of those conversations had ever occurred. He fought to keep his voice even and controlled.

"Graham, you know that the third quarter end date isn't real. We have huge risks in this project because we're running a massive parallel study in fifty-five countries. If we keep the third-quarter end date we will have to back-pedal in the future. That's going to look a lot worse than setting a new delivery date now. But there's a bigger issue than our public image. We tell the teams that we are interested in true status. We tell them we want aggressive project plans. We tell them we want to get rid of all the padding in these tasks and mini-milestones. If we suddenly start pushing the unbuffered end date as the delivery date for the teams, we're going to lose all the trust we've developed in the last few months. They're going to start padding more than ever, and you'll be worse off than before."

Stephen looked at Graham. "Graham, I know we pushed everyone very hard for that third-quarter timeline. Early on, we were told that it wasn't realistic. But we thought it was just the usual negotiations going on. I think we even changed the project leader and installed someone who was willing to commit to the Q3 deadline. You remember?"

Graham was already processing his next steps. He remembered exactly what Stephen was talking about. This would be a major announcement, though. He had to inform the board and then rephrase the script for the analyst call. This quarter's numbers looked good, and he had hoped to give Altus's stock price a little push. Now he had to figure out how to soften the blow.

"How many projects have we re-planned so far?"

Mike answered quickly: "As of noon today, we have fourteen projects scheduled, plus FOX7".

"If we don't take FOX7 into account, what's our average cycle-time improvement according to the new plans?"

"It's a range of about fifteen to fifty percent cycle-time reduction." Mike was relieved that his habit of tracking those numbers in real time meant that he knew them cold.

"Okay. Here's what's going to happen. We will announce Critical Chain on the next analyst call. We're going to highlight our cycle-time reduction of—say, conservatively fifteen percent—on strategic assets. Then, we'll say something to the effect that as part of our strategic realignment we are going to accelerate fourteen key assets across the board. As a result, we are repositioning FOX7 to come on to the market in the second quarter of the year after next."

Graham's assistant was taking frantic notes. "And get Kathy to rephrase that a bit so it sounds nicer. Stephen, I expect you to give them two minutes on Critical Chain. That should do it. Now, let's talk to the board first."

Graham didn't have time for more. He nodded at Mike and left in a hurry. Mike didn't mind. Graham was running a relay race too.

Fortunately for Mike, who was fairly sure that he was under some serious scrutiny from Graham after the revelations about FOX7, the analyst call went well. There were a lot of questions about Critical Chain. The bad news about FOX7 was noticed, but the distractions of the improved cycle times and the new project management system meant that it didn't turn out to be a scandalous announcement.

The next day the stock market headed up slightly, because some new employment data in the US, Germany, and the UK showed signs of improvement. Even Altus Labs' stock price went up a little, although not as much as its competitors.

Mike just kept working.

Chapter 14

THE BOTTLENECK

*I*t's amazing how real things become once people see something on TV. Initially, the people in network builds were a bit hesitant to commit fully to Altus's new Critical Chain approach. Some team members didn't want to give up their padded durations. Others loved multitasking, because it made them feel needed. Certain doubts had been raised that Critical Chain was just another management "flavor of the month" that would disappear as quickly as it came.

The company-wide emails from Graham had helped. Also, all Steering Team members had thorough conversations during their staff meetings. But nothing made a bigger impact than a few interviews with Graham,

Stephen, and some project leads, all of whom shared their early experiences with Critical Chain on Altus Labs' TV channel. The interviews were shown multiple times over a period of two weeks on the monitors that were stationed all over the Altus Labs campus. Afterward, Critical Chain wasn't one more improvement initiative at Altus Labs anymore. It was "the way we do it from here on out."

A call from Sandy at 5.45 A.M. woke Mike up a bit earlier than usual. "I'm sorry to drag you out of bed, Mike. I had a bout of insomnia tonight. Wanted to finish up our preparation of the Steering Team slides. I went into our new enterprise Critical Chain software and looked up some data. I found something that I need you to come over and see for yourself."

"All right. Do I have time for my workout? Or is this pressing?" Mike knew what her answer would be.

"Just come over!"

Mike knew Sandy didn't mess around. She certainly didn't have a tendency to panic. If she'd gotten him out of bed, it was for a very good reason. He got ready as quickly as possible, stopping only to get some coffee on the way. Thirty minutes later he was in the Critical Chain war room. Obviously, Sandy had spent the night there. He was a bit surprised to see that Bob Gabriel had also shown up. They both greeted each other with a short nod.

"If you managed to get both Bob and me here while it's still dark out, you must be worried. Who did you call first, Sandy?" Mike feigned some wounded managerial pride.

She smiled. "I plead the fifth."

"Well, at least I have my coffee. What's up?"

"Well, Mike, you might find this interesting. I was working on the status slides for the Steering Team on Friday. While putting the data together, I looked at the Critical Chains of our projects. All fifteen of them. I printed them out and started to color code the functions on the Critical Chain. I used yellow for tox, green for regulatory, brown for manufacturing, red for clinical operations, and blue for project management."

It was then that Mike noticed the print-outs of the Critical Chain on the back wall of the room. They looked like a rainbow. A rainbow with a lot of red.

"It looks like there's a lot of red—a lot of clinical operations stuff on the Critical Chain. Did you quantify this already?"

"Yes. Take a look at this spreadsheet. If I take all the tasks that are on the Critical Chain and map it to their respective function, Clinical has ninety-three percent of those tasks.

Mike was astounded. "Let me get a look at that." He stared at the spreadsheet for a minute. "Bob, what do you think?"

Bob hadn't even looked at the screen. "I'd say nobody's going to be surprised. If you include all the studies in there, everybody knows that Clinical drives the timeline. That's what we do here at Altus. There is little you can do about the length of a study. An eight-week rat study is an eight-week rat study. A one-year trial is a one-year trial."

Mike said, "Okay. What if we take the actual studies and all other non-compressible tasks out?"

Sandy nodded and started to modify her analysis. Within a few minutes she had new data where they could see it. "Here we go! Even if I take those out, clinical operations is on the Critical Chain about seventy-five percent of the time."

Mike looked first at Sandy, then at Bob. "I think we've got a bottleneck."

Now Bob started to look at the screen as well. There had always been a lot of bickering in Altus Labs about why everything was always so late. Some people had pointed Mike toward clinical operations. But almost as many kept talking about how inefficient regulatory was. Others said that science just takes time. He hadn't paid too much attention to any of it initially. The padded durations and endless games of Schedule Chicken were enough to tackle at the outset. But this was important.

Mike leaned over the screen. "Sandy, that's a really interesting finding. Let's go over the data one more time.

I want to make sure that this is solid. I'll have one of the consultants go over the data independently today. Just write me a quick email to let me know where the files are. And go home and get some sleep. We're on this."

Sandy typed up her results. Later that day Mike received a call from the consultant. The data were correct. Seventy-five percent of the Critical Chain tasks were owned by clinical operations. Eight percent were regulatory. Four percent were toxicology. Nine percent were manufacturing and the final four percent were project management. Mike knew he had an interesting Steering Team session ahead of him on Friday. But this was not data he could just dump in his report. He had to call Charlene first. He had her mobile on speed dial.

"Charlene, do you have a minute?"

"Sure. What's up?"

"I have some interesting data for you. We did a bottleneck analysis based on the existing Critical Chain schedules. It seems we have strong evidence that Clinical is driving the timeline for most projects."

"Well, I am not surprised," Charlene responded. "How did you track this?"

Mike explained to her how they mapped the Critical Chain tasks back to the respective functions.

"Listen, Charlene. I could show up with this report at the Steering Team meeting and introduce everyone to these findings at once. However, I think it would be nice if you reach out to Joseph, to at least tell him that this is coming. That should help us have a more useful meeting, instead of just making him mad."

Charlene agreed. She promised to review the high-level data with Joseph prior to the meeting.

Mike's slides were sent out to the Steering Team on Thursday around noon. Mike didn't want to spend a lot of meeting time reporting on status itself. Each of the projects was discussed on one slide. They showed the current committed date as compared to the previous date. There was a fever chart for those projects that were in execution. It showed the Critical Chain for each particular project. There was a risk analysis that identified project-specific risks and mitigation strategies. And finally he had a checklist on team performance, to confirm that teams were planning and executing using the correct processes.

Charlene and all the functional VPs were at the Steering Team meeting before Mike even walked in the door. He exchanged friendly hellos with Craig Mollestun, the head of Altus's toxicology organization; Kim Young, the head of regulatory affairs; Gerd Schmelting, the head of manufacturing; as well as Joseph McCullen, head of clinical operations. He looked so calm that Mike wondered for a minute if Charlene actually had done her call. There was friendly chatting among the VPs about kids, vacation plans, and so on until Graham and Steven walked in and the room began to quiet down.

Mike started the meeting with the portfolio status updates. His charts were part of a weekly portfolio report that was shared in Altus Labs up and down the organization. It helped to zero in on critical issues. It allowed for some thorough feedback for the teams and for upper management. The Steering Team was already used to the new format and discussed escalations that were brought to its attention. After about forty-five minutes, Mike captured the action items and decisions that were made. After all those issues were dealt with, Mike used the rest of the time to discuss the bottleneck analysis.

"Let's switch gears for a second. The other night we analyzed which tasks on the Critical Chain belong to what function here at Altus Labs. We wanted to understand to what degree tox, regulatory, manufacturing, clinical operations, and project management are on the Critical Chain. You'll find that analysis on page twenty of the report and up here on the screen."

It was just one slide. One slide with a lot of implications.

"The result is very interesting. It's rare to get such clear proof of the existence of a bottleneck. But we do have one. Seventy-five percent of all Critical Chain tasks are owned by Clinical Operations."

Mike looked over at Joseph McCullen. Nobody would have liked to hear this. While it did highlight the importance of Joseph's department, it also clearly indicated that his group was largely responsible for Altus's delays. As he pointed this out, Mike knew he still had four friends among the five functional VPs. The question was how Joseph would take his discovery.

Graham looked over at Joseph, joking, "I always said that you really anchored this company. I just didn't quite mean it like that." There was a little chuckling, more because of nerves than because of Graham's joke. But everybody knew that Graham thought highly of Joseph. He had taken over clinical operations three years ago and made some good progress. Graham had actually given Joseph an award last year.

Fortunately, Joseph was a scientist trained to deal with data all the time—good or bad. He mentioned that he and Charlene had already begun talking about this prior to the Steering Team meeting. He asked a few questions about the methodology of the analysis.

"I assume you took out the time it takes to perform the long Phase III clinical trials. Because there is really nothing we can do about those."

Mike confirmed that. He also explained that they had taken out any task that all by itself was non-compressible:

healthy volunteer studies, the dose-ranging studies, and the long-phase efficacy and safety studies.

"That makes sense." Joseph replied. "I'm not surprised that we are on the Critical Chain that often. After all, clinical operations is a key component in the R&D process. Having said this, though, there are a few things that I observed over the last few years that could be a part of the puzzle."

He paused for a second.

"Over the last three years we have been looking for various ways to get better across the entire company. As a result, there were a number of initiatives conducted by our Six Sigma group. I got some complaints from my folks that some of these process improvement projects weren't helping, but we still spend a lot of time supporting them. I also think we have some key roles that are understaffed. We have been, as a company, very cautious about adding extra resources. Maybe it's time to revisit these decisions.

"Mike, I also have a question for you. It's one thing to know about a bottleneck. It's another thing to have a plan for fixing it. What do you think we should do?"

Everything that Joseph had said made sense. Clearly he was not a VP who just played defense. He had certainly seen Mike's slide, thought about what it meant, and thought about the reasons behind it. Mike had, too, and he was glad to have an answer for Joseph.

"I think you're right. We have already made a solid impact with better planning and moving teams to a relay race mentality. Detecting this bottleneck is an additional opportunity for improvement. Here's what we can do. The schedules we have put together so far track the work involved in a project only far enough to keep the project networks manageable. I think we need to conduct a deep dive into your operation. Let's take a look at the key handoffs. Where do we lose time? Where can we accelerate? Where do we encounter delays because of insufficient resourcing? If we can answer those questions for clinical operations, we'll have the keys to further acceleration. We also need to take a look at all the Six Sigma initiatives and verify that they can help us address the bottleneck. We need to get lean. We need to get our work right the first time. Our Critical Chain plans will tell us what areas we need to focus on."

Joseph was smiling. "I'll buy that. Streamlining our Six Sigma efforts and making sure they coordinate with Critical Chain should make my life much simpler. When can we start?"

Stephen was sitting back in the room. He and Graham had sponsored many of these Six Sigma efforts. Stephen had put a lot of pressure on the various process improvement groups to come up with efficiency suggestions. He was more than a little worried that Mike and Joseph were about to go overboard in their excitement. Trashing Six Sigma wasn't the way to solve the bottleneck. "Mike, I'd be interested to capture what we learn here. Would you mind if I invited the Six Sigma group into this exercise?"

"Not at all. If we can identify the key processes in Joseph's organization, we'll need all the help we can get to come up with new ideas or better approaches. But we might find out that less is more here. There might be only a handful of key initiatives necessary. I think having the Six Sigma people there would be a great way to focus what we already know about process improvement."

The meeting adjourned and Mike and Joseph headed rapidly for the Building One Starbucks to do some real planning.

〰〰

With the bottleneck meeting scheduled for Monday, Mike was ready, finally, for the weekend. He grabbed his overnight bag and drove quickly to the small airfield where the Altus Labs Gulfstream was waiting.

"Ready to go, Sam? We've got a big weekend ahead of us. Can't wait to get there."

"Me neither, Mike. It's been a while since I've really had a chance to cut loose. My fingers are getting itchy just thinking about it."

Mike settled back into his seat and spent the flight reviewing the bottleneck issue and thinking about the most productive ways to try to address it. That, and a quick nap, got him back to California in no time.

Sam brought the Gulfstream in for a landing at a private airfield outside the city. When the door opened and Mike stuck his head out into the bright sunshine he was greeted by Tim, his friend Will from the support group who proudly showed Mike how well he was managing on his new leg, and five more of Tim's best friends from the support group, all bouncing around like kangaroos on speed.

Tim ran up to give him a giant hug. "This is going to be the best birthday ever!!"

Mike agreed. "You guys ready to leave? Everybody got your permission slips? Everybody got your non-disclosure agreements? Because my boss will kill me if this shows up on the news tonight! Hug your folks and let's get going!"

The kids managed to hand over their paperwork to Mike—who hadn't been kidding—say goodbye to their parents, and tumble onto the plane. Mike made sure they were buckled in good and tight, gave Sam the thumbs up, and they were off.

What Mike hadn't quite mentioned to Sally when he'd told her the plans for Tim's birthday was that Sam was a former fighter pilot, stationed in Dayton, Ohio before he flew for Altus, who couldn't think of a better way to cheer up a bunch of kids with cancer than to take them for something a little more exciting than the average plane trip. And that's exactly what Sam did. He flew the Gulfstream to a small private airfield in Nevada, unloaded Mike and the kids, and took them up again, one by one, in the smaller, livelier, Citabria he'd borrowed from a friend of his.

After each of the kids came barreling off the plane, exploding with the excitement at the tight turns they'd taken, the chance they'd had to take the controls, Mike insisted on having his own turn. He looked down from the plane window at the riotous crew of kids on the tarmac. He knew he'd never forget this. He knew they never would either. He knew that the odds were that some of them wouldn't be around for more than one or two more of their own birthdays. But he also knew that kids were experts at beating the odds. Look at how well Tim was doing. Look at Will, who was hoping to pitch for his baseball team again next summer. He looked. He looked long and hard.

Back on the ground again, Mike gave Tim a quick wink and got an incandescent grin in return. Then he and Sam ushered the kids into the hangar for long enough to have some cupcakes—decorated with airplanes, of course—and ice cream, and for everyone to get a set of pilot wings and a hat and thoroughly check out the cockpits of both planes. Sam, who like most military pilots prided himself on being tough and untouchable, completely melted when the kids told him that this was the coolest, most awesome thing they'd ever done, and that he was, obviously, the greatest pilot ever.

With the kids all full of cake and ice cream, Sam wisely made the flight home as smooth as possible. The quiet flight didn't matter one bit to the kids, who were busily replaying each dip and turn they'd experienced. And it didn't matter to Mike, who was pretty sure he'd be grinning about this until Tim's next birthday, at least. And it didn't matter one bit to Tim, who assured his dad that no one, ever, in the whole world, had ever had a better birthday.

The icing on the birthday cake that day was coming home from the airfield to find Sally waiting with the results from Tim's most recent MRI. Beaming through her tears, she silently handed them to Mike. Clear. The scans were completely clear. There was no visible tumor. It didn't mean Timmy was cured, but it meant Supragrel was working. He was getting better. That was a birthday present worth waiting for.

Chapter 15

PICKING UP SPEED

One Monday evening in early May, when Mike stopped in to Building One to pick up his final Starbucks of the day, a project manager motioned him over surreptitiously and asked Mike if he'd heard the most recent rumors about clinical operations. Apparently the whole company was buzzing with the news that clinical operations was on the Critical Chain a whopping seventy-five percent of the time—more than any other function in the whole company. The guys from clinical operations seemed simultaneously proud and terrified of being that important. Everyone else seemed vaguely relieved that it wasn't them. Mike was just entertained to watch it all getting worked out around him. He'd been pretty sure this would be the gossip at the end of the day.

That morning, rather than presenting their bottleneck status as a problem, Joseph had pitched it as an opportunity for clinical operations to make a substantial positive impact on Altus Labs' company performance. That same afternoon, he scheduled a review of all the improvement efforts that were active. There were twenty-seven separate initiatives. At the end of the day, only five of those were allowed to continue. The Critical Chain deep dive into the clinical operations was one of them. Joseph canceled twenty-two projects that had kept almost two hundred and forty-five people busy for a least of a portion of their time.

Quietly chuckling at the speed and accuracy of the company rumor mill, Mike got a call from Joseph filling him in on the details of his review, calling special attention to the projects he'd cut and the people he'd freed up.

"I've been wanting to do this for ages," said Joseph. Mike laughed out loud.

"Good job. That's how you create capacity. Kill a few projects. And pretty soon, we'll find out where we're getting held up and we'll know where to put all those extra people you've just found."

Joseph said, "You show me what's on the Critical Chain and I'll make it faster."

"I plan to. See you tomorrow at the network build."

The next morning they started a three-day network build designed to go deeply into the details of the clinical project management process. They had two clinical project managers in the room, a clinician, two writers, two representatives from the data management group, representation from finance, four representatives from affiliates in the U.S. as well as Europe and Asia, and a Six Sigma Black Belt who had successfully worked on a number of process improvement initiatives in Joseph's organization.

Until now, the Critical Chain plans had only tried to capture the most essential parts of the work conducted in Joseph's organization. Sandy had put together the straw man of a schedule based on the team's existing work. She then spent the morning doing basic training in all the key concepts for the project team so that everyone would know what was going on. That same afternoon, the group put more detailed tasks into the network, outlining processes for finalizing a protocol, data capture, site enrollment, budgeting, and so on. At the end of the day, Sandy led the team through a thorough overview of the work that was required to start up a study. They captured all the crucial tasks, including the enrollment of patients. The team was exhausted.

When the meeting was adjourned, the sighs of relief rapidly turned to groans when all the participants were asked to come back the next day at 7 A.M. sharp. Sandy didn't mind the complaints. Her days in IT had taught her how to deal with ornery colleagues. She ignored them. She was on a mission. Mike liked that.

The next morning the group began reviewing the plot of the network while getting the essential dose of coffee as well some doughnut-shaped carbs. By 8 A.M. they were all in agreement. The network was valid. It was time for Sandy to compute the Critical Chain from Study Start Up to First Patient Visit or "FPV" as they called it.

Mike and Joseph were curious to see what the new Critical Chain would look like and how the team would react. When the chain went up on screen, Joseph put his glasses on, a sure sign that he was interested. After looking at the Critical Chain and the buffer for a bit, Joseph was the first to comment.

"It looks like it will take us a hundred and ten days to get to FPV. That is not bad, but still . . . " said Joseph, "It doesn't change a lot for us."

Mike digested the chain himself. In the meantime Sandy was walking the group through some key tasks on the Critical Chain. She asked, "Here is a question for the group. I just looked up what happens after protocol approval. It seems there are a slew of activities that are dependent on getting the protocol approved. Is that really the case?"

"That is standard operating procedure." The comment came from the clinician, who was nodding sagely, convinced that he just said the right thing. Apparently he hadn't been paying attention to all the signs that standard operating procedure wasn't going to be good enough any more.

Joseph cleared his throat and then said, "Wait a second. We don't need a fully fleshed-out and approved protocol to start working on the site selection, budgeting, or data-capturing process. We have a good idea, pretty early on, of what those key components of a protocol are going to look like. We could start that work earlier."

The Six Sigma Black Belt weighed in. "I know we analyzed projects in the past where we didn't follow standard operating procedures. The teams had some sort of synopsis of the protocol—enough for them to get moving. Based on that, some of the work that normally occurs after protocol approval was started earlier. We had the feeling that it could help to improve communication and potentially move us a bit faster. We didn't pursue the idea further because the project manager caught a lot of heat at the time for doing that. But I think Joseph is right. We could simply define a step called 'study synopsis.' Using that synopsis, instead of a full protocol, we can start budgeting, site selection, and data capturing earlier. It's certainly workable, but how much is it going to help?"

"There's only one way to find out," Sandy said.

She gave most of the group an hour break to do email and catch up with voice mail. With the help of Joseph, the Six Sigma Black Belt, the clinician, and one of the clinical project managers, she modeled the changes.

After an hour the team came back and reran the Critical Chain analysis. It was astounding, but they'd just found a way to reduce the whole process from study startup to first patient visit by twenty-five percent. Joseph was delighted.

They were on the right track. After three more days, Sandy had pushed the team to the maximum. They had turned over every corner of clinical operations. They had found even more improvement potential, though the study synopsis idea was by far the star of the show.

Sandy was able to demonstrate a thirty-two percent overall time improvement for this one key process. Altus Labs was running between seven hundred and eight hundred clinical trials in a given year. Every single trial had to go through this process. This was a significant finding. This had broken the bottleneck. This was what Critical Chain did best.

After Sandy's network build was over, Mike sent her home for a well-deserved weekend of rest. He told her that if he so much as caught a glimpse of her before Monday morning, she was in big trouble. Then he asked one of the consultants to put in a little time over the weekend simulating the impact of this improved process on the company's portfolio.

~~~

Mike wasn't sure, as he stepped off the Gulfstream, whether Tim's rapturous greetings were for him or for Sam. He knew that Tim and Sam spent about a quarter of an hour going over Sam's logbook and flight plans and talking about how old Tim had to be before he could take flying lessons.

They were still elated about the MRI results from Tim's birthday, but another one was coming up soon. Mike wondered if he would ever stop feeling that terror in the pit of his stomach when Tim went in for a test like that. He wondered if he was always going to be bracing himself to hear another doctor tell him bad news.

He looked over at Tim, laughing and chatting with Sam, and caught Sally's eyes as she leaned indulgently up against the car, waiting for her guys to be ready to join her. He decided, for now, to stop worrying about what was coming next. Right now looked pretty good. And right now, he wanted a pizza and a movie with his two favorite people.

~~~

The following Monday Mike met Graham, Stephen, and Joseph for lunch in the executive dining room on the twelfth floor. Joseph had sent an ecstatic email about Mike's help that prompted the invitation. They served *prosciutto e melone* as an appetizer with *saltimbocca a la romana* to follow. The meal made Mike remember the years he'd spent at one of Versa's Italian manufacturing sites north of Milan. The Italians had lunch every day like there was something to celebrate. Though Mike was pleased with his progress so far, right now he wasn't really in the mood for any kind of celebration. Not yet.

"So Mike, Joseph said that we found the ultimate turbo boost for Altus Labs."

Joseph stepped in to add eagerly, "Last week, I had the most productive meeting I've had here in a decade. We are going to be able to reduce the front end of our clinical trial process significantly. This means we will be able to start the enrollment process faster for hundreds of studies every year. This is huge. Turns out that with the new process clinical operations is on the Critical Chain only forty-two percent of the time. Manufacturing and other functions show up more on the Critical Chain now, too. Mike and I were talking, and we think it's time to call the other functional VPs. This kind of targeted analysis would make sense for their areas too. What happened with clinical operations is not a one-off thing, and it's not limited to that particular function. It looks like we'll be able to repeat that kind of improvement on any process from here on out."

Mike tried to downplay his pleasure in the outcome a little, because it was starting to sound like a beer commercial. Next thing he knew, someone was going to try to hug him.

"All we did was let people talk. If you do that, they find better ways to do things. Then, we can simulate the impact real time. Seeing the improvements right away gave the team focus in their ability to solve the problem."

Stephen, scientist that he was, asked a pointed question.

"Right. So you've simulated it. What do we have to do to make it work outside the computer?"

Mike cleared his throat and took a sip of water before answering that question.

"I think we have a much clearer front-end process now. We have some work to do, to update our standard operating procedures and to clear out some of the process clutter. In the short term we will get a big bang just by reorganizing the work according to our findings from last week. But ultimately we need to make sure that behavior here is truly in line with Critical Chain. This is all about focus. If a task is on the Critical Chain, then we need to get it done. We need to move the results to the next person on the Critical Chain. We need to run the relay race while operating with a high level of quality—that's what has to happen. But I need all of you to make that work. I can't be the only one pushing the teams."

Mike took a bite of saltimbocca and waited to hear what they'd say.

Graham leaned back in his chair. "I already know what I'm going to do about that, Mike. You've shown me how much slack we've been carrying around here, and you've shown me how much faster we can go. So here's what's going to happen. We're cutting that slack. We're cutting the buffer. The focus task estimates are the new mandatory goals. No exceptions. And we're going to make sure that our performance plans are explicitly tied to those goals." He raised an eyebrow, looking very pleased with himself.

Mike choked. Clutching his glass of water he tried to regain his breath and his temper before laying into Graham and explaining, yet again, the crucial importance of the buffer. Just as he began to calm down enough to speak, Graham, Joseph, and Stephen burst into laughter.

Mike raised his hands in surrender. "Okay, you got me."

Once they'd stopped commenting on how red he'd turned, and then how pale, and once Mike had decided to forgive them, they got back to business. They were in agreement. It sounded simple, but, just like Mike had said in the boardroom briefing, so does weight loss. Burning more calories than you eat and getting some exercise on a regular basis isn't a difficult concept. Yet half of the U.S. population is obese. Everyone knew that Altus Labs needed to change. They all knew that if Altus Labs wanted to survive, it had to become lean and fit, and it had to stay that way.

"Changing behaviors is the most critical thing," Graham agreed. "Those old habits and old games are what got us in trouble in the first place. So we've got to get rid of them. How do we do it?"

"I thought it was great for Joseph to be there at the meeting last week. That showed his team that he—and for that matter all of you—were behind this. Making tough decisions, like canceling some of the Six Sigma projects to make time to focus on the real problems was a great signal, too. People knew that you want Critical Chain to be a priority and that you care about their work situation as well. Ultimately, success will breed success. Let people hear what we're getting out of this. Let them see what they'll get out of it. Make it known."

As Mike took a sip from his cappuccino, he had no idea that Graham was already planning to do exactly that. And more.

Chapter 16

THE WORD GETS OUT

*U*nlike the semiconductor industry where Mike had spent most of his career, where corporations fiercely competed with each other and hardly talked, the pharmaceutical industry was fairly open. Naturally, companies developed competing products. All major pharmaceutical companies had some stake in oncology or diabetes, for example. However, there was also a lot of information-sharing between companies. Mike learned about that when Charlene asked him to give a presentation about "Critical Chain at Altus Labs" in one of the project management tracks at the Drug Industry Association conference. The DIA is a non-profit organization focused on biopharmaceuticals that educates professionals in the Life

Sciences industry, and Charlene was well-connected to one of their frequent session chairs. Charlene got invited to DIA events on a regular basis and had a standing slot at their annual meeting. This time she thought it would be better for Mike to make an appearance there. The average presentation was for thirty to forty people, so it was no big deal for Mike to agree to polish one of his standard Critical Chain speeches for the occasion.

He reviewed the conference agenda carefully. He always did that before agreeing to put himself into the middle of an unfamiliar situation. He liked to know what to expect. It looked to him like the conference was something of a main event for the pharmaceutical industry. It was visited by more than eight thousand scientists, according to the brochure. There were slots and tracks on all aspects of the industry. The event started on Sunday with a welcome lunch, and the rest of that day and Monday were filled with tutorials. Over the next three days there were twenty-four parallel sessions on various topics that filled each day from breakfast until dinner.

Since this year's event was in Washington, D.C., and since Graham was using the company jet that week, Mike decided he could take advantage of some direct flights, give his presentation, and fly right home to California. So he agreed to give the speech. Of course, it turned out that it wasn't as easy as simply polishing an old speech and putting some new slides together. There was a legal review within Altus Labs that everything had to go through first.

To cover every contingency, Mike sent legal all of the one hundred twenty slides he had assembled since he had started to work at Altus Labs. He randomly indicated five slides as his priority choices, and indicated that the rest would be backup. Fortunately, the gambit worked and the whole presentation was approved, though not without the reminder to put a legal disclaimer in the footnotes. That done, Mike decided to wait until he was on the plane to make his final choice of which slides to show.

Mike took the early 6:30 A.M. flight on United, flipping through slides and making decisions on the way. He landed in D.C. at 7:25 A.M. Less than twenty-five minutes later he was in his rental car on the way to downtown. Since his presentation was at 11, there was even time for a quick appearance at Starbucks to truly wake up. As they handed him his cappuccino, he noticed that his phone was out of juice. He'd been running so hard lately that something had finally slipped his attention. He hadn't remembered to charge the phone. It wasn't a big deal. The convention center was sure to have somewhere he could plug in, but until he had a chance to do that he was going to feel a bit isolated from the rest of the world.

The D.C. convention center was in an interesting part of the town—half upwardly mobile and half spiraling down. He drove by a little strip mall with a pawn shop, a dry cleaner, and the quintessential Chinese restaurant. Then the convention center came into view. It had been erected as a modern coliseum for corporate warriors. It had countless conference rooms for groups of every size and was easily able to absorb the several thousand DIA visitors.

Mike looked for somewhere to park and discovered that the best piece of real estate in the city belonged to the toothless man who owned the parking lot just next to the convention center. For twenty-five dollars, Mike was permitted to park his car there for three hours: cash, no credit cards, no receipts. Mike took a second to calculate the guy's annual revenue and whistled softly as he walked into the convention center.

It was 9:55 A.M. With his presentation whittled down to the right five slides on the memory stick, he was ready to go. His flight to California would leave at 2 P.M. from Dulles Airport. He had to be out of there by 11:45 A.M. to make it to the airport in time. So, this had better be quick.

At the registration table, Mike checked in as a speaker and picked up his badge. As he pinned it in place, the professionally perky lady at the table told him that the meeting had been moved to a different conference room due to a last-minute request. The track would be held in Auditorium B. She added, somewhat nervously, that it was a really nice room, and really so much better suited for his needs. She smiled at Mike, who barely noticed it.

Mike had about thirty minutes left before his session was scheduled to start. His session chair had asked him to see him beforehand in order to go over how he would like to be introduced. Mike also wanted a chance to go through the slides and deal with any last-minute arrangements or tech issues, so he went straight to Auditorium B. It was much bigger than he had expected. It would easily hold two hundred people. What the heck were they expecting to happen here this morning?

Right behind the speaker podium, Mike found an outlet and finally had time to plug in his phone. He noticed a call from Charlene that must have come in while he was in the air. He'd have to call her back on the way to the airport. There was no time now.

People were already pouring into the room when Mike shook the hand of the session chair for the first time. The session chair was a friendly junior exec from GlaxoSmithKline. Mike found out that he worked about ten miles from Altus Labs' offices in Chesterton. They went through the slides together and didn't find any problems. Mike got the usual speaker's instructions and signed some documents, so that the slides could be published later on. He let the session chair know that he had to leave right after the presentation. He'd only have time for one or two questions: He had a plane to catch. The session chair smiled and commented that he understood. Given the latest news from Altus Labs, he'd certainly guess that Mike was going to be very busy.

Mike had no idea what that was supposed to mean, so he ignored it and watched the room fill up to capacity. Mike remembered that Charlene had described this as a presentation for thirty to forty people. It looked to Mike as though he was going to have more than five times that many in the audience. It didn't make a difference to his presentation, but he surely hadn't expected two hundred people to come look at his five slides. He would definitely mention this when he finally had a chance to call her back.

When his name was called, Mike stepped quickly to the podium. On stage, he looked at a fully occupied Auditorium B. Two hundred faces he had never seen before. He smiled at the group and let them know that he was pleased, if surprised, to see so many people there. Then he swung into his presentation. He gave an overview of the basic concepts of Critical Chain and then picked a few examples from Altus Labs to demonstrate how the methodology worked in practice. His jokes and anecdotes worked where and when he wanted them to. He received friendly applause at the end. People liked him. It was one of his strengths as a speaker. Deep down, he enjoyed those moments, but today he just wanted to find the shortest way to get out of this room, get into the airport, and get to California.

When the Q&A session started, the session chair reminded the audience that Mike had only time for one or two questions. One of the younger guys, clearly full of motivation and curiosity, somehow managed to get from his seat halfway to the back of the room and make it to the microphone first. "Mr. Knight. Thanks for the great speech. But I guess that, like me, most of us are here because we read this morning's article in the *Wall Street Journal*. So I'm guessing that everyone wants to know the same things that I do. How long has Altus been using Critical Chain, and what exactly triggered the decision to use it as the sole project management methodology across the entire company?"

Mike had no idea what this kid was talking about. What *Wall Street Journal* article? What did he mean by "sole project management methodology"? Mike decided to play it safe and give a non-answer as an answer: "Altus Labs has a policy of keeping speakers on a pretty short leash. You all know how it is." Some people chuckled. "I can only answer questions directly related to the specifics of my presentation. Perhaps we can talk off-the-record later."

People at the DIA were very friendly to each other. Well-educated scientists don't step on each others' toes. Someone asked Mike a standard question about buffer management and how executives reacted to the existence of buffers in a schedule. Mike gave him his standard answer: that executives needed to be trained like anyone else to understand the purpose of the buffer and that, with good training, this rapidly became a non-issue.

After some more thanks and another round of applause, Mike picked up his phone, but he couldn't listen to his message from Charlene because he couldn't get out of the room without being intercepted by people who wanted to network with him. He felt a bit like a rock star. And he had no idea why. It would have been fun, if mystifying, except that he needed to get going. He kept the conversations as short as he could and gave out every business card he had on him. Someone was even nice enough to give him a copy of the *Journal* to take on the plane.

On his way to the airport, Mike finally had a chance to listen to Charlene's voicemail. She'd given him a heads up on the article and warned him that she expected some questions would come up as a result of it. As usual, she knew exactly what she was talking about. Apparently, Mike had some important reading to do on the plane.

∧∧∧

Enjoying the only perk of his frequent flier status that meant anything to him, Mike boarded the plane before everyone else, stowed his bag, and settled into 1D, his favorite seat. As everyone else followed him onto the plane, fought over luggage space, and tried to get drinks from the flight attendants, he took out the *Wall Street Journal* and started reading. There was Altus Labs, right on the front page, getting a brief reference in the "What's News" column under "Business & Finance." Surely that wasn't what all the fuss was about! Mike quickly flipped through the rest of the paper. There it was. Front page, second section. Apparently Graham had given the *Journal* an exclusive interview.

Mike asked the flight attendant for a cup of coffee and started reading.

WSJ: You shared some mixed news on a recent analyst call. One of your major new developments for diabetes treatment, FOX7, was delayed. But offsetting that, you also reported significant timeline improvements across your major drug pipeline. Can you give us some more background on this?

Graham Fletcher: We are in the same boat as every other pharmaceutical company these days. It is becoming tougher than ever to find blockbuster drugs and take them to the public. We all have a harder time getting our drugs through the regulatory process. Every year it takes longer to get approval from the FDA here in the U.S. The picture doesn't look much different internationally. There's also an aggressive generics industry that replaces any drug whose patent has expired. So the cost of developing just one new drug is quickly approaching 1.5 billion U.S. dollars, while our average revenues per drug are decreasing annually. The ways that we have always managed the research and development process are not appropriate anymore. Altus Labs has to change. Everyone has to."

WSJ: "So, Mr. Fletcher, how will Altus Labs deal with these challenges?"

Graham Fletcher: "There are three major parts to our strategy for tackling these challenges. First, we need to find innovative ways to identify promising molecules. In the past we have focused primarily on candidate molecules that our own researchers came up with. We recognize, however, that there are more researchers on this planet than we can hire. So we are systematically strengthening our relationships with companies and research institutes in biopharma. For example, here in the U.S. we will invest in strategic relationships with companies in the biopharma hubs in Southern California and in the Boston area.

"Second, we need to be disciplined in the way we spend money. Altus Labs owns a lot of real estate. Most of the buildings we operate in are owned and operated by us. This includes manufacturing sites as well as office buildings. We will be taking a hard look at our current assets and deciding which ones we really need. We have also identified a number of strategic outsourcing partners that can take over essential parts of our manufacturing and R&D process, giving us more flexibility and a better cost/benefit ratio.

"Third, we found that our in-house development of drugs can be profitably accelerated by state-of-the art project management methodologies. We have been testing a project management methodology called Critical Chain that is superior to the management approaches we've used in the past. With it, we've been averaging acceleration rates of fifteen percent and higher on our projects, while meeting our commitment dates close to one hundred percent of the time. In addition, Critical Chain improves the communication among project team members. And it has vastly improved the visibility of the true project status at the executive level."

WSJ: "Why didn't it help you with FOX7? Didn't you just give that a later delivery date? Where's the double-digit acceleration?"

Graham Fletcher: "Critical Chain helped us discover early on that the original commitment for FOX7 needed to be revised. The original timeline we had communicated was based on scientific assumptions that have since been disproved. We had to revise those. We're confident that with Critical Chain we will find the fastest way to bring this drug to market. The results that we see on all of our other drug development projects speak for themselves."

WSJ: "What is so different about Critical Chain?"

Graham Fletcher: "The pharmaceutical industry is actually a latecomer here. Critical Chain is a proven method that is already used in other industries. The core principles are simple. Critical Chain is all about focus. We want our scientists to focus their work on critical and time-sensitive tasks. Once that is done, the output of that task is handed over to the next person. We liken Critical Chain to a relay race for knowledge workers. While we are running a race, we all want the team to be focused on what is important. Critical Chain is able to show us what is most important across our entire portfolio. That is probably the most significant difference compared to what we had before."

WSJ: "What kinds of projects are you managing with this methodology?"

Graham Fletcher: "Eventually, we will manage all of our projects with this approach. Critical Chain will be the sole project management methodology at Altus Labs. We are still in the process of converting some of our R&D projects, but I expect this to be completed soon. I have asked our CIO, in charge of Altus Labs IT, to make plans to roll out the methodology to the rest of the company once we are done on the R&D side. We are also reviewing ways to use this approach to work with our strategic outsourcing partners in the future."

WSJ: "So, what is the bottom-line impact of Critical Chain, in your estimation?"

Graham Fletcher: "The acceleration of our most strategic assets is worth billions of dollars to us. You can imagine what will happen when we begin to see that acceleration throughout our entire portfolio. We're also going to see our drugs shipped to our patients more quickly. We are going to be faster to market, and we'll have the potential to help more people and help them more efficiently. Moving forward, we are better-positioned to fully develop drugs that we would not have marketed otherwise, because there was not enough patent time left for us to make it work. Because we are able to accelerate, we are better-positioned to take calculated risks. Again, in the end our patients and our shareholders win. Those are the people we care about most.

WSJ: "What investment level is necessary to make this work? Will we see an increased head count as a result?"

Graham Fletcher: "Our hard-money investment is very low. We funded the implementation costs out of our allocated budgets without any significant increases. We won't have to increase our head count as a result. The main cost—if you want to call it that—is our determination to adopt a lean way to manage projects. I would compare it to a weight-loss program for an entire corporation. At Altus Labs, we decided to run a relay race. You don't see overweight relay racers at international track meets. We compete with other leading pharmaceutical companies on a worldwide level. We decided to drop weight and become faster. Critical Chain helped us to understand the best ways for us to do that.

WSJ: "Exciting times at your company. What will the share price be a year from now?"

Graham Fletcher: "I wish I knew. Hopefully higher. Have you heard something?"

WSJ: "Mr. Fletcher. We thank you for your time."

〰〰

Mike folded the paper and slid it into the pocket of his bag. Double-digit acceleration, focus, sole project management methodology . . . it was clear that the treatment was working. Altus Labs was transforming rapidly. The company was on the way back to health—leaner and more nimble. Mike couldn't wait for the flight to end.

Chapter 17

COMING HOME

*T*he first thing Mike did when he got home from the airport after the DIA conference was unpack. Less than twenty-four hours later, he would be packing again. But instead of packing to head back to his small apartment in Chesterton, or for yet another business trip, he was going to be packing at home with Tim and Sally for ten perfect, glorious, work-free days on Kauai.

Before that, though, he had one important meeting left.

The next morning he, Tim, and Sally all gathered in front of the webcam, opened up Skype, and placed a call. Dr. Hart's smiling face appeared and they all leaned in to see.

"It's great to see all three of you again! Mike, it's been too long. Tim, how are you feeling? Sally, you're looking like you might finally be getting some sleep."

Dr. Hart seemed to be trying to catch up with all of them at once as she adjusted the angle of her webcam, the volume on her speakers, and waved hello. Mike gave her a chance to get coordinated and said, "Hi, Dr. Hart. We thought it would be nice if we all got to listen in this time."

"I'm glad that you did. I want to compliment all of you, all three of you, on how well you've gotten through this. For Tim to be so ill was an enormous challenge for him—as it was for both of you. On top of that, Mike took the job out of town . . . a lot of couples couldn't have survived that kind of strain. And a lot of kids would have struggled enormously. You've all held together really well."

Sally blushed, looking pleased. "I think that having the support group to turn to really helped. You should see all the letters we've gotten over the past months. And knowing that Mike was only gone because he was working as hard as he could at Altus to help Tim while I worked as hard as I could at home really made it feel like teamwork, you know?"

"I do." Dr. Hart took out the ever-growing folder that held Tim's chart. "But of course it was Tim who did all the work. Right, Tim? It's not like your parents got their brains sliced open, is it? So let's take a look at how you're doing."

Mike couldn't breathe. God, how had Sally gotten through any of these meetings or conversations without him? He was a pretty tough guy, but he was pretty sure that if she wasn't holding his hand right now, he'd be heading out of the room to throw up from nerves.

Then Dr. Hart smiled.

"Kiddo, this is one beautiful brain you've got here. You see this MRI?" She held it up to the camera as she spoke. "We talked about this last time, right? This is where the tumor was. We got most of it with surgery. And then the radiation got some more. But you know what? This is your third clean MRI in a row. I bet your Dad's brain doesn't look this good. And I bet when I see you again in three months, the picture's going to be just as pretty. Nice job, Tim."

She nodded to him as solemnly as if he were a fellow surgeon and turned her focus to Mike and Sally.

"He's doing great. The results from the Supragrel are as good as we could have hoped for. I don't see any residual tumor at all—neither did any of the colleagues I called in to doublecheck the scan. He's had limited side effects from the drug and seems to have virtually none from the surgery. This kid of yours is going to be fine. He's not at the end of this, but he is at the beginning of being a kid again instead of a patient. Take him home. Treat him normally. Ground him if he blows off his homework. Let him play sports. Just bring him back every three months for an MRI so I can keep an eye on him.

"Now, do me a favor, you three? It's been great working with you, but please . . . don't need me again, okay?"

Sally joyfully and tearfully agreed that they'd do their best to keep everyone from needing Dr. Hart's services for as long as possible. As for Mike, he figured he'd stop hugging Tim in just a little while. Like when he left for college, maybe.

~~~

Sam's voice came over the intercom. "Okay, Knights, we're on our way. Don't forget to buckle up until we're leveled out. Everyone says it's a perfect day for a flight to Kauai, so just sit back and relax and I'll have you there in no time. Not sure what I'll do with my best co-pilot riding in the back, though. So Tim, you come on up here and say hi if you get bored with your folks, okay?"

And they were off. The minute the plane leveled, Sally looked at Mike and Tim. "I'm sorry guys. I've got to get some sleep if you want me to be ready to hit the beach when we get to Hawaii. But you two can have a little guy time. There hasn't been a lot of that lately."

Kissing them both, she flattened out her seat, curled up under a blanket, and promptly sacked out. Mike knew her exhaustion was as much from the release of tension after the good news from Dr. Hart yesterday as it was from all the long hours she'd been putting in lately with Tim and the support group and everything else. And he and Tim were happy to have the guy time. He'd promised Tim pretty much unlimited chessboard hours over vacation, when they would finally have the time for some serious playing. Now here they were, with a whole flight's worth of time in front of them, and days of vacation time after that. And, according to Dr. Hart, a whole lifetime's worth of time to look forward to.

"Why don't you set up the chessboard, buddy? We'll see if you've learned any new tricks."

An hour later, it was clear Tim had learned more than a few tricks. The chess he'd been taught as part of his therapy had rapidly gone from therapeutic exercise to entertainment, from entertainment to a hobby, and from a hobby to a serious sport. Tim, frankly, wiped the floor with his dad.

And then he did it again.

When they were 3 to 1 in Tim's favor, Mike pleaded for mercy, enjoying his losses nearly as much as Tim was enjoying the wins. Mike promised to do some real practicing with the computer to try to become, as Tim put it, "a worthy opponent." They ate a few sandwiches, watched part of a movie, and then Tim went up to the cockpit to say hi to Sam.

Mike stretched out next to Sally to get some sleep, asking Tim to wake him when they got close to landing. He didn't want to miss that view.

When Tim shook him awake a little while later, Mike woke Sally as well. They raised the shades and looked out. The shockingly blue waters of the Napili coast and the almost vertical rise of the jade green cliffs from the water into the sky were a sight that had amazed Mike and Sally on their first trip here, and sharing it with Tim was an extra pleasure.

"Dad! It's the cliffs from *Jurassic Park*, right?"

"They are. No dinosaurs this time, though."

No dinosaurs. Mike wouldn't have worried, though, even if there had been. They'd already fought worse monsters, and won.

Chapter 18

EPILOGUE

When they got back from Kaui, the Knights moved into their new house near Altus Labs headquarters. Tim continued to use Supragrel for another twenty-four months and his MRIs remained clean. There were no signs of the tumor. The illness had affected his coordination skills slightly; ball sports like soccer and basketball were more difficult for him than they had been before. So the Knights decided to take up running as a family. They regularly participated in events like "Race for the Cure" and other charitable runs. Dr. Hart wrote a number of papers about Supragrel in which Tim's recovery was cited. Twice a year she spoke to other kids with similar conditions as a spokesperson at hospitals around the country.

Tim developed an interest in everything that had to do with brains. How do they work? How do humans think and learn? He was fascinated by their variety and their seemingly infinitely complex plasticity. He'd been building a model of the brain on his desk and stayed in frequent contact with Dr. Hart and his therapist to talk about neurology. He was talking about becoming a neurosurgeon.

Tim continued to beat his dad at chess regularly. Mike didn't mind. He was simply happy that Tim's brain continued to develop and learn beyond levels that Mike had thought were realistic. The story of his son kept him going at Altus Labs. There was a lot of work that needed to be done and a lot of people to be helped.

Mike continued the rollout of Critical Chain at Altus Labs. It took the company another twelve months to move the entire portfolio to the new methodology. It wasn't long after that when they began the next level of improvements for Altus: using their Critical Chain schedules to improve resource management, plan for needed resources, and identify new bottlenecks.

Altus Labs decided to extend Critical Chain to their partner base as well. Doing business with Altus Labs meant that a partner had to get up to speed on the Critical Chain methodology. Mike developed a specialized curriculum for these partner companies and oversaw the rollout.

After Critical Chain had been successfully put to work at Altus Labs' R&D organization, the CIO of Altus Labs, Ram Gupta, approached Mike. Neither one of them had forgotten their initial, somewhat hostile exchange in the boardroom. But that was history. Ram admitted that projects in IT were hardly ever on time and that this was for reasons not much different from the ones in Altus Labs' R&D organization. Ram was no longer a skeptic; he wanted to bring Critical Chain into his organization as well. Mike put a team together for the IT organization. After twelve months, the on-time delivery rate of Altus Labs' IT projects was well above ninety percent.

Today, hanging on the wall of Mike's office is the baton first used by the Supragrel team. It is signed by everyone who held it and handed it off. Beneath it is a picture of Tim standing next to Sam and Mike after his first flying lesson.

IMPLEMENTING CRITICAL CHAIN

Case Studies

At ProChain, we have conducted Critical Chain implementations in a number of different verticals. Our customers are in the high tech, pharmaceutical, medical device, consumer product, aerospace, and defense industries. Naturally, everybody thinks they are different. "What works in high tech can't possibly be working in pharma." Or, "What works in the aerospace industry can't possibly work for us in the consumer products industry. Right?" I hear that a lot. Please allow me to let you in on a secret. We have applied the same principles across all these industries, we have used the same standard processes to manage projects, and we have used the same set of tools—off the shelf, no customization.

Here is a selection of companies that have implemented Critical Chain successfully. What all these cases have in common is that the same solution helped them to overcome their project management issues. This solution has three components:

1. A common set of tools used across all projects, including a standardized process to manage projects based on Critical Chain principles and a Critical Chain software platform enabling the entire enterprise.

2. Certified Critical Chain experts and project managers.

3. A trained workforce including executives, functional managers, and individual contributors.

Case 1

Fortune 200 Pharmaceuticals Company: New Product Development

Initial Situation: Like almost any other pharmaceutical company today, this client is facing a dwindling pipeline and more competitive market. Like at Altus Labs, their milestone management system caused significant inefficiencies. As a result, this company met its major milestones only about forty percent of the time. The implementation of Critical Chain was designed to deliver projects on time and to gain both efficiency and speed.

Results Achieved: Within two years, the entire portfolio was using Critical Chain. On-time completion of projects is reported at one hundred percent. Key processes were reduced significantly. In particular, speed improvements in managing their clinical operation were upwards of forty percent. A senior leader stated: **"This [Critical Chain] is a key part of our strategy for long-term success."**

Case 2

Fortune 1000 Medical Products Company: Multiple New Product Introductions

Initial Situation: This organization was meeting their major milestones only about twenty-two percent of the time. There was a clear lack of priorities between the projects. Individual contributors were required to work extensive overtime in order to complete projects. Project schedules were too detailed to be managed practically.

Results Achieved: In this implementation, we helped to schedule more than thirty top-priority projects. The on-time completion of projects increased from twenty-two percent to well above ninety percent. The ROI is conservatively assessed at 500:1. One Senior Manager stated: **"We're obviously less stressed and more effective."**

Case 3

Fortune 200 High Technology Company: New Product Introductions

Initial Situation: The project scope was routinely decreased in order to meet project due dates. Overall, the company faced poor product quality. Deadlines were hit because people worked significant overtime toward the end of projects. Some of the root causes for this situation were non-trivial changes to project requirements during the project without knowledge of their impact, and overly aggressive and unrealistic schedules. As a result, the company frequently missed key promised dates. Only ten percent of projects delivered on time.

Results Achieved: Projects now completed on time in an environment where everything had been late. Schedules are now believable and credible. A senior program manager said: **"ProChain Project Management is now a critical part of our operational methodology. The ROI for this implementation of PPM is ludicrous."**

Implementation Phases

A Critical Chain implementation is done in two major phases: The Pilot Phase and the Rollout Phase. Each of these phases contains a Learn phase and a Confirm phase. The key objective of the Learn phase is to understand the causes and effects of suboptimal project execution. In the Confirm phase, the team uses the Critical Chain Project Management processes to overcome these deficiencies.

Phase I: The Pilot

The Pilot elements are shown in Figure 2. The main objective of the Pilot is to learn how the principles of Critical Chain and the Critical Chain Project Management processes and tools apply in the particular organization. The Pilot also shows the efficacy of the overall approach.

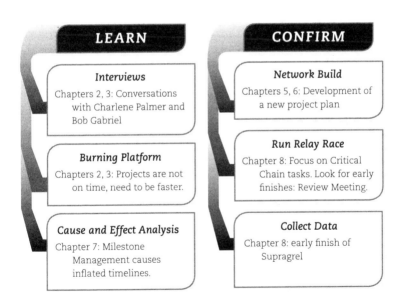

LEARN

Interviews
Chapters 2, 3: Conversations with Charlene Palmer and Bob Gabriel

Burning Platform
Chapters 2, 3: Projects are not on time, need to be faster.

Cause and Effect Analysis
Chapter 7: Milestone Management causes inflated timelines.

CONFIRM

Network Build
Chapters 5, 6: Development of a new project plan

Run Relay Race
Chapter 8: Focus on Critical Chain tasks. Look for early finishes: Review Meeting.

Collect Data
Chapter 8: early finish of Supragrel

Figure 2: Pilot

Phase II: The Rollout

The second phase of a Critical Chain implementation, shown in Figure 3, also utilizes the "Learn and Confirm" approach at an organizational level. In the Learn phase the implementation team completes their understanding of all key objectives of the executive stakeholders. They develop a cause and effect analysis that is based on the Pilot and on additional findings made during the interviews for the Rollout. The burning platform of the Rollout is based on strategic issues that are relevant to the entire organization. Typically, it revolves around a combination of time-to-market, on-time delivery rate, or quality of execution.

The Confirm phase of a Rollout includes a number of key elements. There is a senior-level steering team overseeing the implementation. Its role is to establish the vision of the rollout as well as monitoring its ongoing progress. There is a communication plan that ensures that people within the organization understand the importance of the rollout and its objectives, and are kept informed about ongoing developments. This can also include communication with external stakeholders (e.g., shareholders, scientific community, etc.).

During a rollout, it is critical for an organization to move its entire portfolio to the Critical Chain project management methodology. That helps minimize the

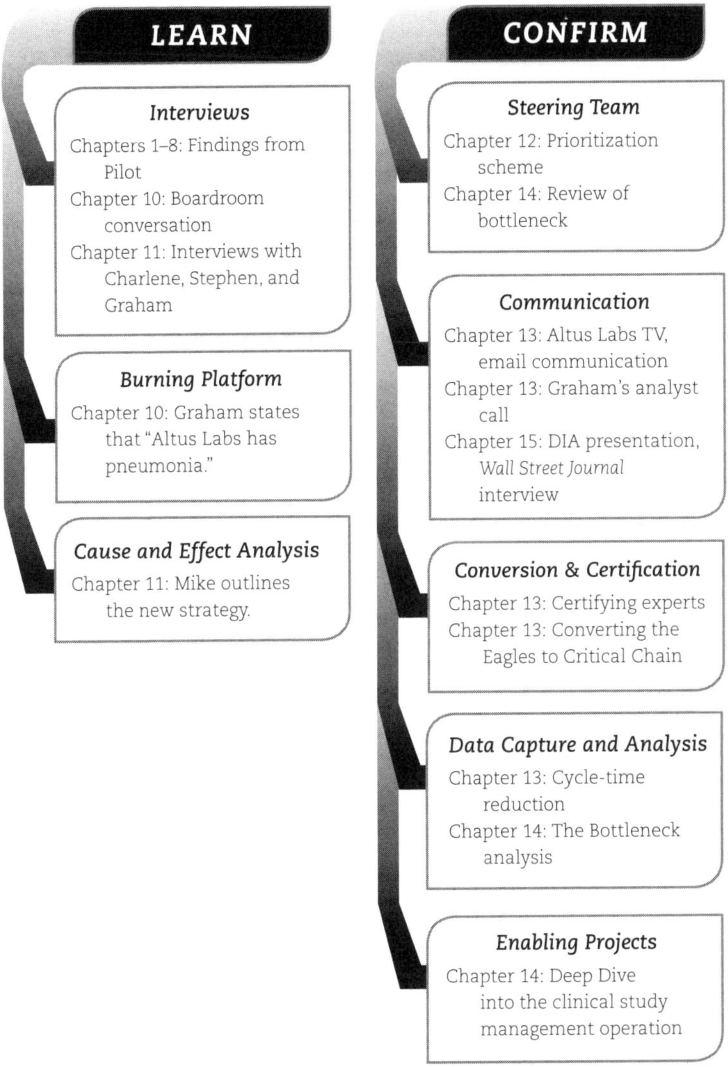

LEARN

Interviews
Chapters 1–8: Findings from
  Pilot
Chapter 10: Boardroom
  conversation
Chapter 11: Interviews with
  Charlene, Stephen, and
  Graham

Burning Platform
Chapter 10: Graham states
  that "Altus Labs has
  pneumonia."

Cause and Effect Analysis
Chapter 11: Mike outlines
  the new strategy.

CONFIRM

Steering Team
Chapter 12: Prioritization
  scheme
Chapter 14: Review of
  bottleneck

Communication
Chapter 13: Altus Labs TV,
  email communication
Chapter 13: Graham's analyst
  call
Chapter 15: DIA presentation,
  Wall Street Journal
  interview

Conversion & Certification
Chapter 13: Certifying experts
Chapter 13: Converting the
  Eagles to Critical Chain

Data Capture and Analysis
Chapter 13: Cycle-time
  reduction
Chapter 14: The Bottleneck
  analysis

Enabling Projects
Chapter 14: Deep Dive
  into the clinical study
  management operation

Figure 3: Critical Chain Rollout

disconnects that can come from different ways of working and helps maintain momentum toward adopting the new approach. In addition, as project schedules are developed for the entire portfolio, the organization and its internal experts gain important knowledge about the approach, ensuring that the organization can independently execute the Critical Chain methodology. The certification approach ensures that projects are planned and managed on a weekly basis in a consistent way. Project teams are following a consistent process and report status based on a common set of indicators.

We strongly advise our clients to capture on an ongoing basis key metrics such as on-time delivery rates and cycle times. As the organization increasingly understands what processes are holding up its work, improvement initiatives—so-called "enabling projects"—are launched to further improve the operation. Ultimately, the Critical Chain approach becomes the lynchpin of the new relay race approach that brings not just the immediate benefits experienced by Altus Labs, but more and more benefits into the future.